OBJECT LESSONS

Stephanie Kane

COLD HARD PRESS

Denver, Colorado

Automat

"Kane delivers yet again for fans of fine art and whodunnits."

—*Kirkus Reviews*

"*Automat* is an intriguing mystery, and you will also learn a lot about artist Edward Hopper."

—*The Denver Post*

"*Automat* is an intense drama that keeps you at the edge of your seat."

—*Starry Constellation Magazine*

"Wonderfully disorienting."

—*Cereal At Midnight*

A Perfect Eye
A Denver Post Bestseller

"An artistic thriller that will keep readers guessing and please the author's fans."

—*Kirkus Reviews*

"Come for the setting, stay for the story. An absorbing mystery set in familiar territory. A bonus: you learn an awful lot about art restoration."

—*The Denver Post*

"This is really one of those books you can't put down. It is both an enlightening and wonderfully told inside story of the world of art curators and forgeries and a gripping thriller. You wonder why you didn't see the ending coming, which is truly the mark of a compelling and skillfully told mystery."

—Harry Maclean, Edgar Award Winner and #1 New York Times Bestselling Author of *In Broad Daylight*

"Lily Sparks' keen powers of observation and Stephanie Kane's snappy, hard-edged writing make for a highly original mystery that provides a whole gallery full of heart-pounding chills."

—Mark Stevens, Author of the Allison Coil Mystery Series including *The Melancholy Howl*

"A great mystery story that is page-turning. I loved the story and actually finished it in a few hours."

—*Celtic Lady's Reviews*

"The story is full of intrigue and draws you in. A good murder from beginning to end."

—*Hello Booklover*

Seeds of Doubt
Colorado Authors League Award Winner

"Kane deserves to join the ranks of the big-time legal-thriller eagles."
—*Publishers Weekly*

"Kane's background as a defense attorney informs the legal thriller backbone of the story, but the exploration of childhood sins, whether monstrous or incidental, gives *Seeds of Doubt* its emotional heft."

—*The Baltimore Sun*

"Deftly written."

—*Chicago Sun*

"One of the outstanding mysteries of the year."

—*The Cleveland Plain-Dealer*

Extreme Indifference
Colorado Book Award Winner
Colorado Authors League Award Winner

"Sturdy intrigue in and out of court with an especially sharp eye for the riptides of power running just beneath the legal quiddities."

—*Kirkus Reviews*

"Fast-moving and intriguing. Kane knows both her protagonist and the legal terrain well."

—*San Francisco Chronicle*

"A tight, well-written thriller with an ending that caught me completely off-balance."

—*The Cleveland Plain-Dealer*

"A fast-paced satisfying ride. The novel's climax is heart-stopping, and its conclusion just right."

—*The Denver Post*

"Stephanie Kane writes legal thrillers that are on a par with John Grisham and Scott Turow."

—*The Midwest Book Review*

Blind Spot

"The protagonist of Kane's debut legal thriller has the makings of becoming the law profession's answer to Kinsey Milhone."

—*Publishers Weekly*

"Riveting stuff. Kane reads like Jane Austen. The truth she finds in the end is both stunning and, in retrospect, entirely obvious."

—*The American Bar Association Journal*

Quiet Time

Also by Stephanie Kane

OBJECT LESSONS

First Edition
First Printing, 2021

Cold Hard Press
Denver, CO

Interior design by Susan Brooks
Cover design by Marcel Venter

Library of Congress Control Number: 2021903745

ISBN Print: 978-1-7336715-7-6
ISBN Digital: 978-1-7336715-8-3

Printed in the United States of America

For John

A small thing may give an analogy of great things, and show the tracks of knowledge.

—Lucretius, *De rerum natura*

"Miko!" she called.

She waited for him to jump up on the bed. Had she forgotten his kibble? She gave him another moment. When she turned the swivel-mounted TV on, the nightlight flickered and her irritation grew. Par for the course. Bill wired it. *Gratitude, gratitude...* she reminded herself.

Sipping her chamomile tea, she surfed the news.

Sunday evening was feel-good stories. A couple in separate nursing homes celebrating their seventieth by Zoom, a gal in Britain hatching ducks from a carton of grocery store eggs.

"Miko?"

If he was punishing her, he couldn't be far.

In slippers she padded to the railing and looked down. Except for Miko, all was in its place. Everything in her domain sparked bliss: kitchenette off the cozy den, clawfoot basin in the bath, nook with fold-down desk for her laptop. What she'd kept of her old life spoke to her heart, and she wasn't about to lose it to an asshole who wired a lamp to a TV.

"Mi-ko—"

A strange scent overtook the chamomile.

She descended the ladder and checked the stove's burner. Off, but Bill had just replaced the propane. Did he fuck that up, too? *Gratitude, gratitude.* Him no longer cluttering her life was enough. Now the smell was stronger, acrid—chemical. From outside.

She shook the little container of kibble.

"*Mi*—ko!"

What Miko really wanted was a field mouse, preferably blended. The mini-Keurig on her counter took up too much space to have a Vitamix, but cats were hunters. Had he been inside when she came home? Through the window a full moon glinted off the *For Sale* sign. Bill and his lawyer thought they had her over a barrel, but she'd come out on top. Soon he'd be out of her life for good.

A movement caught her eye. Something furtive—a fox, or worse a coyote?

She pulled on her rubber gardening boots. Heedless of her thin robe, she unchained the door and rattled the knob. It stuck. Trust him to install a cheap one. She turned harder and the knob came off in her hand. She stepped back and took two deep breaths. *Gratitude...* She pushed the door with both hands, then threw her hip behind it.

Through the window a torch flashed. Twin jets glowed ice blue.

The stench was overpowering.

She flung herself against the door.

The tiny house exploded.

Chapter One

"What'd I miss?" Lily whispered to Paul.

The burly men shuffling around the object at the front of the room looked more like schoolboys needing to pee than seasoned Denver homicide cops.

"Eve Castle has a tough crowd," Paul murmured.

But the petite brunette who was addressing them seemed unfazed. She wore a black sheath with ballerina sleeves, and an impressive diamond glinted on her left hand. "What do you see?" she asked the men.

"Dead girl," grunted a paunchy cop.

Eve nodded. "Very good, Detective…?"

"Johnson."

"And what else is hiding in plain sight, Detective Johnson?"

A couple of plainclothes guys snickered.

Lily glanced at her phone. A dozen calls. If only she could snicker away what waited in plain sight back at the lab, or the chaos at her condo since Paul had moved in. He saw her with the phone and shook his head. *Even here?* his look said.

Ping. Another text—

The room fell silent and she looked up. Despite themselves, the brawny detectives had stopped shuffling. A crime scene was a world within a world. A miniature stage where a killer played God simply defied them to look away.

Lily moved closer.

The dead girl was wedged between a fold-down bed and a couch with overstuffed cushions. Flossy golden hair and knees tucked to her chest made her seem doll-like, but her face was contorted in a distressingly real cry. A calico cat crouched at the foot of the bed.

"Who was she?" Eve asked softly.

"Paralegal," Johnson began. "What do you call 'em now—"

"Demi," Eve said.

"—*legal assistant* at a fancy downtown firm."

"How did Demi die?"

"Asphyxiation. How do I know?" Johnson pushed his glasses up on his forehead and pretended to peer at his notes. "Her face is blue!"

Guffaws broke the spell.

Lily squeezed past the men to the front of the crowd. She couldn't help staring either. A girl's universe had been shrunk to this tiny moment, her birth announcement and obit on one page.

Eve scanned the audience. "What does Demi's apartment say about her?"

"No room for a guy," a cop said.

"Hell," another called out, "not even space for an adult!"

He had a point.

Minimalism was the new norm. A 300-square-foot micro-mini studio was for busy millennials who wanted a place to sleep, stash clothes and microwave a meal. The tall ceiling provided vertical storage and the bay window airiness and light, but the *For Rent* sign spoke to high turnover, a developer unashamed to charge a ransom for such tiny digs, and young professionals squeezed at both ends on their climb up the ladder. Like Lily's own apartment when she'd been a brand-new associate at her fancy law firm two careers and a lifetime ago, Demi probably thought this was heaven.

Paul joined her. "Bet you had one just like it."

"What?" Lily replied.

"The Krups."

How sophisticated her old Krups had seemed! Just as she herself used to do to get to her desk early, Demi had set out a travel mug and teed up the coffee machine. Demi's Krups was silver, with a red power button and gleaming glass carafe.

A beetle-browed rookie reached for it and marveled, "Geez, it could fit right in my—"

Lily bumped his hand away.

A perfect little lawyer suit hung in Demi's closet, and low-heeled pumps were lined up on the floor. Prosser's *Law of Torts* lay face down on the couch. Demi had even set out kibble for her cat. *She could be me,* Lily thought.

"Facts," Eve said.

"Demi leaves work and goes to Union Station's Oyster Bar," Johnson replied. "Picks up a guy, the sex gets rough, he panics and stuffs her behind the couch."

"Or she's getting it on with a married partner," one of the older cops said.

Lily winced.

That too.

"Another headache?" Paul whispered sympathetically.

"Look at her cases," Johnson demanded. "If she's banging a partner, maybe she was planning to file an @MeToo!"

Eyerolls and groans.

"Assume nothing," Eve warned. "Observe."

Law school treatise… suit and coffee… kibble. Lily glanced at Paul. He wasn't getting it either.

"Back to the crime scene," Eve said. "What doesn't stand out?" She gestured and her ring flashed, the diamond seeming to float in its silver-grey band. "Anyone?"

Ping. Ignoring her phone, Lily looked at Paul again.

He shook his head. This was Johnson's show.

To hell with Johnson—and the lab. She locked eyes with Eve. "The cat."

"Where'd you get it, anyway?" the rookie asked. "It's so—"

"Was the cat hiding when the first officers arrived?" Lily asked.

"No," Eve replied, "he was exactly where he is now."

The shuffling and fidgeting stopped.

"Swab his claws," Lily said.

Johnson snorted. "Claws? Demi's lucky it didn't munch her face. Cartilage crunches like a pig's ear!"

"He's got plenty of food." Lily pointed to the kibble. "He's guarding Demi's body. If there was an intruder, maybe he clawed him."

Eve's eyes gleamed. "You said *if,* Ms...?"

"Sparks," Lily said. "No outcry?"

"What?" Johnson said.

"The neighbors are right on top of her," Lily said. "And check for antihistamines. I bet Demi had asthma."

The room was completely silent.

"Demi didn't bring home a date," Lily continued. "Her sheets aren't mussed and the light's still on over the bed. Go back to the Oyster Bar and see what she ordered—probably a takeout. She was cramming for an exam."

"But—" Johnson began.

"She slipped and got trapped between the bed and the couch."

"*Huh?*"

"You nailed it, Johnson," Lily said kindly. "Positional asphyxia. Demi weighed what, 90 pounds? Those pillows are as big as she was. She was reaching for the law book and got pinned between the pillows and the bed frame. Her lungs and diaphragm were compressed, and allergies make it harder to breathe. She was a victim of radical downsizing."

"Bravo, Ms. Sparks!" Eve cried.

Johnson slapped his forehead. "Allergies? She had a damn cat!"

Eve arched her brows questioningly at Lily.

"Cat lovers always put them first," Lily said.

—

"We meet again, Ms. Sparks," Johnson said.

"Thanks for letting us come." He'd invited Paul, not her.

Johnson gestured good-naturedly at the two-by-two-foot diorama on the conference room table. "Hell, it's just a dollhouse."

They both knew it was far more than that.

Every crime scene was a microcosm of depravity, but shrinking one to the ratio of an inch to a foot reduced evil to a scale where you could understand it. The tiny objects in Demi's micro-mini studio were perfect replicas of their life-sized counterparts, each begging to be touched or played with. Who could blame that rookie for reaching for the Krups? Lily herself itched to open the miniature Prosser. And Demi…

"Unh-uh," Johnson warned.

Just in time, Lily stopped herself from adjusting the doll's robe. Bendable plastic had no modesty, and she had no business tampering with a crime scene, fabricated or not. According to the Denver Police Department's handout, the precursors to Eve Castle's diorama dated back to the 1940s, when Frances Glessner Lee, heiress to a Chicago farm equipment fortune, first created miniature crime scenes as a training tool for homicide investigators. Now Castle Training was the hottest thing in criminal justice, with police departments around the country vying for DOJ grants for custom-designed dioramas to hone their own detectives' skills. Paul had helped Johnson draft DPD's proposal.

Now Johnson winked. "You knew all the answers, Ms. Sparks. Did somebody slip you a cheat sheet?"

"She didn't need to cheat," a voice said. Turning, Lily saw Eve Castle had joined them. She held out her hand to Lily. "Denver Art Museum's Conservator of Paintings, right?"

"Till six months ago," Lily replied. "I've gone in-house at The Kurtz Foundation."

"Angela Kurtz," Eve murmured, "how lucky for you both. I've heard about your perfect eye, Lily. After tonight, I see what they meant."

Johnson wagged his finger. "Watch out. Ms. Sparks attracts real killers like catnip. And speaking of cats—"

"Your diorama is genius," Lily broke in.

"The genius was Frances Glessner Lee," Eve replied. "Her crime scenes were composites of real cases, with clues so contradictory they couldn't be solved from visual evidence alone. She wanted detectives to look for markers of social class and state of mind. To up the ante, the witness statements she wrote were sometimes false."

"Welcome to my world," Johnson muttered.

"Miniature crime scenes seem a strange passion for an heiress," Lily said.

Eve chuckled. "Not if you knew Frances' parents. They were more devoted to each other than to her, and they were obsessed with their house. It was a fortress, with few windows facing the street and the ones in the basement barred. They built her and her brother identical townhouses down the street."

"How dreadful!" Lily said. Johnson rolled his eyes and left to join Paul. "How did Frances get into crime?"

"A Harvard friend of her brother's was a medical examiner." Eve shook her head in admiration. "Frances' composites were grisly, even squalid, but she was ahead of her time in more ways than one. Before they became mass-produced toys, dollhouses were designed to teach girls how to run a house. By making domestic scenes deadly terrain, she turned the notion of a dollhouse on its head."

From across the room, Paul waved and pointed to his watch. He was flying to D.C. first thing in the morning and Lily hadn't even thought about dinner. But the idea of a frustrated heiress flipping the script intrigued her. "Did Frances build the dioramas herself?"

"A carpenter did," Eve said, "but Frances designed them and made the dolls. She knit their stockings with straight pins. Why, they even wore undergarments!"

Lily laughed. "Who builds your dioramas?"

"My husband's the architect." Eve's eyes twinkled. "I commit the crimes."

"Big or little?"

Eve grinned. "I write the scripts."

The crowd around the diorama was starting to break up. Johnson clapped Paul on the shoulder, and the beetle-browed rookie sidled over and said something that made everyone laugh. Eve saw Lily watching them. "Generous of you to credit Johnson with solving the case."

"He's a good sport," Lily replied.

Eve sighed. "I missed the cat. Sometimes he slips one past me."

"Johnson?"

"No, my husband. Every clue means something." Paul was coming over, and she patted Lily's arm reassuringly. "Don't worry, there's always takeout. Can I ask you something?"

"Sure."

"What was the tip-off?"

"The Krups," Lily replied, "and Prosser. Demi was in night school, not bringing a guy home from a bar."

Eve squeezed her arm. "And if it were a real murder?"

"Real?"

"Play along," she said. "Say you're Frances Glessner Lee—or the killer—and Prosser was left for a reason. What is it trying to tell you?"

Lily put herself in Demi's low-heeled pumps. "That she had to be stopped."

"Why?" Eve pressed.

Prosser wasn't just a step up the career ladder. It was an aspiring lawyer's passport to freedom.

"Demi was on her way up. And out."

Chapter Two

Lily poured Jack some kibble and rummaged through the fridge. Eggs.

"Scrambled or fried?" she asked Paul over her shoulder.

"Didn't the two of you ever eat real food?" he replied. Who knew Paul liked to cook? Lily tried to ignore the spatters on the stove's backsplash, but he followed her gaze. "Think Abstract Impressionism," he said apologetically. The red splotches did resemble a Pollock. "Your dad and your cat both liked my spaghetti."

"They'll eat anything if they're hungry enough." She cracked an egg off-center and fished pieces of shell from the bowl. Spaghetti sauce on the wall was one of the many surprises since Paul had moved in. Lately he'd been threatening to make five-alarm chili.

Jack crunched down hard on his kibble, and Lily blinked away the image of Demi's cat munching on her ear. Damn Johnson! Paul gently took the fork from her hand; the eggs were whipped to a froth and he'd have to settle for scrambled. And if he made chili she'd have to buy a fire extinguisher.

"How's the lab?" Paul asked.

Which had been crazier, leaving the museum to run Angela Kurtz's state-of-the-art conservation lab, or thinking two adults could share one bath? Fifteen years ago, this condo had been a giant step up from Lily's old studio apartment overlooking Cheesman Park. Her law firm's partners had lived across the way, in mansions and penthouses overlooking the Botanic Garden, and with Dad's bungalow finally behind her and flush with her first paycheck, she'd been so excited to have her own place that she hadn't even read the lease. Now she threw some butter into the pan. "I'll microwave us a couple of English muffins."

"Wow! OJ, too?" Paul slipped his arm around her waist. "Maybe we can have dinner in bed—or skip it entirely."

Lily looked up at him. If the condo walls weren't paper thin, the box spring didn't creak, and her eighty-year-old widowed neighbor Louise wasn't next door. Their last uninhibited romp had been in Paul's room at The Westin; now the only place they let loose was in the shower. Paul leaned down and kissed her neck. Why did he have to smell so good? Sandalwood, cloves... She kissed him back and made it a long one. His lips were warm and tender, and she felt a pulsing in her chest. On the stove the butter sizzled and spat. "I thought you had a plane to catch," she murmured.

"My deposition was postponed."

"Darn! There goes scrubbing the kitchen and the bath..."

Paul undid the top of her blouse and kissed her lower. Her heart was pounding—

Beep... beep... beep!

A high-pitched chirp filled the kitchen, and his enticing scent was overpowered by something burning.

"Shit!" He fumbled for the stove.

Beep! Beep! Beep!

He grabbed the stepstool and turned the smoke alarm off.

Lily put the burnt pan in the sink and turned on the vent over the stove. Slowly it creaked to life and the smoke began to clear. She got out another pan and put more butter in it. Her heart was getting back to normal. "Nothing like a two-alarm fire," she said playfully.

Paul lowered the flame on the burner and began scrambling eggs. "Did you call a realtor?" he asked.

Lily stiffened. From the outside her building might be a charmless pile of concrete, but her unit's tenth-floor wraparound balcony overlooked Cheesman's pines and the Botanic Garden's Japanese pond. When she'd quit law to pursue a conservation degree, this condo had been her haven and her anchor.

"Maybe we can have a den," Paul continued casually.

She looked up. "You've never said what you want."

"A stove with a modern vent," he said, "and something close to work." Downtown for them both—if she still had a job after avoiding Angela over the Thomas Cole manor house portrait waiting at the lab. "What do *you* want, Lily?"

Not to do mascara while he shaved. "A big bath—or two."

"So long as you're happy." Paul gave her a bite of egg to taste, and she added pepper and a pinch of salt. "Let's eat on the couch."

She was still picking corn chip crumbs out from between the cushions after Sunday's Rockies game with Dad. Jack, too was turning into a couch potato; he'd never used to watch TV until Paul moved in. That afternoon she'd fled to the lab and stared for hours at the two-hundred-year-old painting Angela had promised to the Rensselaer in Albany. Now the corn chips in the couch reminded Lily of the manor portrait's disintegrating paint, and the overstuffed cushions of Demi's diorama—She settled next to Paul and loosened his tie.

"Poor Johnson," he chuckled. "You sure ran rings around the old cop tonight."

"His worst nightmare is being forced to play house."

Paul poured the wine. "He's in a tough position; he has to bring in DOJ programs to motivate the rookies, but everyone knows it's no substitute for pounding the pavement." He put his arm around her, and she snuggled in. "But you sure hit it off with Eve Castle." He chuckled again. "It was like watching a trainer throw mackerel to a seal."

She sat up. "Am I the trainer—or the seal?"

"The trainer, of course!"

Lily laid her head back on Paul's chest. Through the balcony door, lights twinkled on across the park. Maybe they'd sit outside later and watch the moon rise over the pond. If only they could just stay here like this… "How's the new firm treating you?" she asked softly.

Paul sighed. "White-collar crime pays too well. It's all about running the clock."

"Why was your depo postponed?"

"Apparently there's some doubt whether a former FBI Assistant Director who prosecuted terrorists and faced down a killer with a machete can defend a bank president."

"Can you?" she teased.

"Only if he really needs it." Paul smiled wryly. "Actually, his D.C. counsel had to attend a bar mitzvah. And at the office today, all they could talk about is that woman in Highlands whose house blew up."

Lily had read about it in the morning *Post*. The house was over on the hip northwest side of town—probably a grand old Victorian someone couldn't wait to buy and gut. She slipped Paul's shoes off and massaged his feet. He sighed gratefully. "Does your firm represent the insurance company?" she asked.

"Her ex in their divorce."

"Since when does a white-collar boutique do pots-and-pans law?"

"Depends who owns the pots and pans."

He put his stockinged feet on the coffee table, and Lily switched on the lamp. Night backlit the glass balcony door, and in its reflection she saw what might pass for a comfortable married couple. Not the ten years they'd wasted apart, or Paul's scar from saving her and Dad from that machete. She tucked her feet under his legs, and he poured them the last of the wine.

"Now tell me about the Cole," he said.

The decaying 1826 manor portrait loomed. "Somehow I missed the course on consolidating disintegrating ground layers in Hudson River

School masterpieces," she replied.

"Does Angela know?" he asked.

"Not yet."

"She believes in you, Lily." That was half the problem. "You'll figure it out, you always do."

"Paintings aren't murder, Paul."

"Too bad." He laughed softly. "To you, even a phony crime scene's a hit of crack…. Hey, just kidding. Relax!" He pulled her down again and kissed her. The couch groaned.

"Louise—"

"Two walls away."

"Paul—"

His foot hit the side table and the lamp crashed to the floor.

"Fuck." He sat up. "A guy at my firm knows a realtor."

Chapter Three

The Kurtz Foundation lab was in a hundred-year-old sugar-beet warehouse which had cost a fortune to gut and rebuild. Sandblasted brick and an eerily quiet geothermal climate control system protected the art while a skylight and north-facing windows bathed the open floor in natural light. On the easel directly under the skylight sat the Cole. Today, even the painting's proper name seemed to mock Lily.

Like a hangover, *Schuylerhaugh in Late Afternoon* was worse in the morning. "Haugh" was an old Scots term referring to a low-lying meadow in a river valley. Schuyler's manor had neither meadow nor valley, but its portrait's condition was more troubling than its uninspiring composition or grandiose title. Sun from the skylight gleamed dully off the waxy film that was migrating to the painting's surface. The ground—the layer between canvas and paint—was shifting in real time. Unsurprisingly, there was no condition report or any formal record of provenance in the Foundation's archives.

Lily detoured around the painting for an espresso. The lab's sleek Italian machine even ground its own beans, an efficiency she suddenly found irritating. She went to her desk. Two new voicemails from the

Rensselaer, first pleading, then desperate. And one from Angela. *Call me.* Instead, she booted up her computer and went to the *Post*'s website. The woman whose house had blown up was Bliss Byrd. Her husband was an Aspen real estate developer, which explained Paul's firm's involvement—

"Lily?"

She looked up.

Angela Kurtz's asymmetric bob and dark blonde streaks set off her cobalt silk sheath, and her shoes were a bold red. Just a year ago she'd been pushed in front of an SUV by a killer who'd been targeting actresses promoting the museum's Edward Hopper show. Now the only hints of Angela's brush with death and her excruciating rehab were the extra-wide straps of her custom-made Mary Janes and her cane. Its steel tip and lacquered handle could pass for a shooting stick.

"The Rensselaer's carpet-bombing me," Angela said.

She'd promised *Schuylerhaugh* to them to commemorate the 220th anniversary of Thomas Cole's birth. Cole had founded The Hudson River School, the first American style of painting. Far better known for his majestic depictions of Catskills wilderness than manor house portraits, when he was young and broke he'd painted a handful of the latter for room and board.

But Angela was looking at the computer screen. "I knew Bliss."

"Oh?" A reprieve.

"I met her in Aspen years ago, after she'd fled her first bad marriage. Bill Byrd turned out to be yet another control freak, but Bliss was a genius at reinventing herself." Angela shook her head in admiration. "She became an executive coach, then jumped on the decluttering bandwagon."

"Decluttering?" Lily asked.

"If I wanted to improve myself, I'd drink more vodka." Angela sighed. "You know—that Marie Kondo crap. Less is more, except for the process to become a certified consultant, which practically bankrupted Bliss. She was too proud to ask for help, then things fell apart with Bill.... But that's not why I'm here."

Schuylerhaugh.

Angela nodded grimly. "Benjy Schuyler is a distant cousin of General Philip J. Schulyer, and a dear friend of Dad's. Not that George had any friends—"—even Angela had despised her father—"—but being attentive to donors goes beyond schmoozing with them over martinis while I pick their pockets for the combinations to their vaults."

That explained two things: why there was no condition report on *Schuylerhaugh* in the archive, and why Angela was so keen to loan it to the Rensselaer. Loans were a quid pro quo. Lending a major work to a museum allowed the museum to fill a hole in its collection; in exchange, displaying the work burnished its prestige—not to mention jacking up the work's value if and when the donor sold it. This could raise conflicts of interest, but as head of a private foundation, Angela didn't have to answer to a museum's board of trustees. And if *Schuylerhaugh* belonged to a friend, there was even less reason to look too closely at it.

"It's been in Benjy's family two hundred years," Angela continued, tapping her cane for emphasis. "He grew up saluting it every day. If he hadn't bragged about it at The Cactus Club, it'd still be over his fireplace." But smoke could be cleaned from a canvas and hanging it in such a perilous spot didn't explain the painting's waxy bloom. "The Rensselaer invited Benjy as its honored guest." The tapping crescendoed. "He's giving a keynote on growing up in the shadow of a masterpiece and a Revolutionary War general!"

Lily cast about for words. "It's not as... *heroic* as Cole's landscapes."

Angela's cane pounded the floor. "Like a museum, we function on a system of chits, Lily. Friends loan to friends. The Rensselaer's curator is a friend."

"I—"

"Just send the goddamn painting out!"

The climate control system abruptly cut off.

Angela peered at Lily. "What the hell is wrong?"

"I'll show you."

They went to the easel.

Schuylerhaugh's columned portico and dormer windows hinted at a bygone grandeur, and the canvas's afternoon sun filtered weakly through a smattering of hazy clouds. The house dominated the middle ground, but the foliage creeping up on it threatened to swallow it and the painting back into the wilderness.

"Interesting composition," Angela said gamely.

Sparing Angela the stereo binoculars, Lily wheeled over the standing lamps and angled them parallel to the painting's surface.

Angela leaned in and sniffed. "Cornflakes?"

"The ground's breaking up." One good bounce upon landing in Albany and *Schuylerhaugh* could disintegrate.

"You can fix it, right?" Angela asked.

Given six months, a team from the Tate might be able to reattach the paint. Even then, travel could be iffy. And what would it say about Lily if she went crying for help to the conservators at the Tate? She pictured Demi reaching for Prosser only to have her ambitious little hand cut off.

"I know someone good in Boston," Angela said diplomatically.

Art conservator? The partners at Lily's law firm had hooted when she'd resigned to go back to school for her degree in conservation. *What the hell does an art conservator do?*

"Or at the museum—" Angela continued.

"No!" Lily cried. What if her old nemesis Gina found out she couldn't handle the Cole? After all but giving Gina and Director Michel Roland the finger when she'd quit, she certainly couldn't afford to have Angela turn to them now.

Angela's eyes narrowed. "You'll fix *Schuylerhaugh*."

"No—I mean yes! Of course, I will."

"Need help?" Angela asked shrewdly. "I've budgeted an assistant—"

Matt from Lily's old lab? Too inexperienced, and if word got back... "No, just a little more time."

Angela winked. "Well, don't forget you need to write a condition report." Was she insinuating the painting's real condition could be fudged? But between Benjy Schuyler and the Rensselaer, Angela's rep was on the line too. "And bring Elena tonight."

"Tonight?"

"Dinner. There's a fabulous new couple you've got to meet."

Chapter Four

"You look great," Paul assured her.

Lily patted her hair. She'd barely had time to shower and throw on a dress. She never knew who—or what—to expect at Angela's dinner parties. As they started up The Kurtz Castle's paved walk, Paul gave Elena Brandt his arm.

"Will those naked putti in the fountain spout my drink?" Elena asked. The octogenarian gallerist swore by her pearls, which tonight accompanied a silk caftan in a Chinese print. Cataracts prevented her from driving, but her signature red oversize glasses gave her license to do just about everything else.

Lily took her other arm. "The houseman will take care of you."

Elena winked lewdly. "Angela runs through 'em fast enough."

In the two years since George Kurtz had died, Angela had done wonders with his Country Club estate. She'd festooned the 1920s French-style chateau with tiny white lights and replaced the junipers around the fountain with soft green arbor vitae. The leaded windows and weathervane atop the turret remained, but the lights now gave the iron lad chasing a squirrel on his bike a playful look.

"George always did like boys," Elena said.

Lily lifted the brass knocker with the roaring lion's head.

"Overcompensating," Elena stage whispered.

The door opened. A slim man with sandy hair and wire-rims stood there with a pint of Guinness. He wore a polo shirt, chinos, and suede shoes. Was he Angela's new houseman? They weren't called butlers anymore.

"Your ears must be ringing," he told Lily as he offered his hand. A sleek silver-grey wedding band gleamed. "My wife goes on and on about you."

Angela came up from behind him with Eve Castle.

"We meet again!" Eve said. "And you've met my husband, Adam."

Elena snickered.

"We get that all the time," Adam said. "Frankly, it's why we married."

Paul laughed. "I'll have what you're having."

The men left for more beer.

"Chuck wagon's out back!" Angela called after them. "Adam may have a Pritzker Award," she whispered to Lily, "but his Miami condos are dead in the water. He's auditioning to give my castle a face lift."

Lily didn't envy Adam. She followed Angela through the great room, trying not to flinch as they passed the library where George Kurtz had been so gruesomely slain. At the threshold to the sunroom, Angela theatrically paused. The French doors that opened onto the patio framed a table on which a three-foot replica of The Kurtz Castle stood.

"A baby dollhouse like my Granny's!" Eve exclaimed. Quivering her chin with disdain, she dropped her voice to an old woman's disapproving rasp. "Girls' play prepares you for women's work."

But Elena was charmed. "Why, it's perfect for my miniatures show this June. Can I borrow it for Brandt Fine Art's front window?"

Instead of a lion's head knocker, the miniature double-width front door had two small knobs. Grasping them, Angela swung the doors open. Magically lit from within, the dollhouse sprang to life. The cook's pantry had a period-perfect standing icebox and gas stove. The living room had tiny oil paintings in gilt frames and a marble fireplace. Thankfully, the little library was lined with books and not George in a plush upholstered chair with his guts smeared on a celadon-and-gold-leafed wall.

Adam and Paul rejoined them.

"This may be all that's left of this house one day," Adam said wistfully. Peering into the miniature library, he frowned.

"What?" Angela demanded.

"Something's not quite..." Adam set down his Guinness and gently tapped the wall behind an armchair. A tiny recess popped open.

"Jeez," Paul muttered.

Adam grinned. "Now let's see how authentic this baby really is." He led them back to Angela's real library, where the celadon-and-gold walls had been repapered with a grass print, and rapped the wall behind where George's armchair had sat. They heard a faint echo. Gently he probed for a seam. He pushed, and a hidden door opened. A bald baby in a stained smock stared imperiously out.

"Holy shit!" Paul said.

The doll's face was shiny and pink, and its shell-like ears were flush to the skull. Through pouched eyes its gaze was avid, hungry. Its parted lips glistened.

"Is this a trick?" Angela demanded.

Adam laughed. He could afford to; unsold Miami condos be damned, with this little sleight-of-hand he was more than halfway to earning The Kurtz Castle's remodeling commission. "Every house has a secret. Craftsmen used to hide clay pipes and animal skeletons in walls to ward off evil." He turned from the doll to Eve. "What kind is it, honey?"

"A Horsman, from around 1910." The grotesque bald baby didn't seem to shock or repel Eve in the least. "The human form fascinates us, so dolls are our oldest toys. They're even replacing emotional support animals on planes."

"Why, they're better than a pet!" Elena declared. "Always there, and with no needs of their own."

Angela's color had returned. "Well, that demon baby can scare the bejesus out of its next owner. Now who the hell's ready to eat?"

———

"You were in *Architectural Digest*," Adam said as he ladled bisque into Lily's bowl at the patio buffet. "A nice page. They gave me a spread earlier this year."

Lily groaned. "Don't forget *Fine Arts Connoisseur*." The lab had been featured everywhere.

Adam's blue eyes flickered with amusement. "Embrace it."

"Why?"

"*Sic transit gloria.*" So much for glory.

Lily balanced two squares of focaccia on Adam's plate. "Pretty slick, back there."

"Old composition dolls are so lifelike," he said modestly. "Amazing what they did with a little sawdust, glue and paint…"

"Finding it was pure genius. Don't pretend."

Adam shook his head, but she could tell he was pleased. "My work's no different from yours, Lily. Don't art conservators pull rabbits from hats?"

Lily glanced over at the lanai. Paul had saved her the seat next to him. Angela's houseman—her real one—had cleared the appetizers and was pouring wine. Eve laughed at something Elena said.

"Must be fun working with your wife," Lily said. "Whose idea was Castle Training?"

"She's the psychologist, ask her." Now Eve's head was bent to Paul. What were they talking about? "He says you're looking for a new place," Adam continued. "Things a bit cramped?"

Lily blushed. What else had Paul confided over Guinness?

Adam smiled sympathetically. "Relax."

They rejoined the party.

"Thank God for Lily," Eve was saying. "Homicides are such juicy bones, it's tough to convince cops not every death's a crime."

Angela set down her fork. "Maybe it depends on the victim. That idiot Johnson has been pretty damn quick to write off Bliss Byrd."

"The woman in the little house?" Eve asked.

For a second Lily thought they meant Demi's diorama, but they were talking about Angela's friend.

"Glorified RVs," Elena said knowingly.

Adam nodded. "Gas and propane hook-ups can be tricky in tiny houses." He added to Lily, "Evidently Bliss plunked hers in her backyard."

"I warned her not to do that," Angela muttered darkly. "The divorce was already pushing Bill to his limit."

"Is it legal to park a house on a lawn?" Lily asked Adam.

"It's a zoning grey area," he said, "but there are safety and building codes. Neighbors can file complaints."

Elena piped up. "I bet one of them ratted her out!"

Angela turned to Paul. "Houses don't just blow up."

"Sounds like an accident," he said noncommittally. "RVs—"

"I don't care if it was a dumpster or a tin can!" Angela said. "Talk to Johnson," she begged, "Bliss was my friend."

Lily squeezed Paul's hand.

"I'll see what I can do," he said.

After they'd finished the sorbet and espresso, Paul set his napkin on the table. "Work tomorrow." He helped Elena up, and she regally gave Adam her other arm. At the door, Lily saw the men exchange cards.

"Let them," Eve said softly. "He needs a friend."

"Paul?"

"Adam—Paul, too. Don't worry, we've been there." She poked Lily playfully in the ribs. "Who cares about the neighbors? You'll work it out."

Did Paul blab about their sex life to Eve, too? Lily tried not to sound resentful. "It seems effortless for you."

Eve smiled knowingly. "One person always gives up more, or thinks he does."

Paul was waving at her insistently from the door. "We're both so busy—"

"All work and no play?" Eve tsk-tsked. "A good roll in the hay works wonders. Of course, for me and Adam, it was CT that saved our marriage."

Lily couldn't help laughing. "Who came up with Demi's diorama?"

"We brainstormed it together." Eve waved gaily at Paul, then turned back. "Let's make a bet. CT's second diorama is Friday. Solve it and I'll buy brunch."

"Sounds like fun. What's the catch?"

Eve's eyes danced. "Frances Glessner Lee's. Who says it can be solved?"

Chapter Five

When Lily drove up to the lab, a familiar figure was peering into the front window—or trying to. Fortunately, the mesh blinds filtered out prying eyes as efficiently as UV light.

"Gina!" Lily cried.

The museum's Curator of Paintings looked up with a start, then her expression morphed into an officious smile. "What time do you usually waltz in?" Gina asked.

Faking a yawn, Lily looked at her watch. "Nine-thirty sharp." A good hour later than she used to arrive at the museum.

"I almost left."

Damn.

Scouring the building's façade, Gina fixed on the discreet steel plaque that said *The Foundation*. "Poor George!" At the museum, visitors couldn't walk two feet without seeing George Kurtz's name.

Inside, Gina took in the skylight, north windows, and state-of-the-art lab equipment at a glance. At the Leica stereo microscope on the column stand she gave a little gasp. The gas-lift swivel arm had a 300-degree horizontal pivoting range and came with a camera, software, ring light, and cold light source. She turned quickly, but not before Lily saw the envy in her eyes. Now she pointed at the Italian coffee machine. "That's in *Fine Arts Connoisseur*."

"I'd offer you a cup, Gina, but you've obviously tanked up."

Gina sashayed over to the easel. "So this is the painting Benjy genuflects to." She'd been sniffing after the Schuyler collection for years. Dropping her crocodile hobo bag on the floor, she leaned in and wrinkled her nose. Lily held her own breath and hoped against hope. One good sneeze and *Schuylerhaugh* would be breadcrumbs. But Gina just stepped back and sighed. "Poor Angela."

"Beg pardon?" Lily replied.

Gina's smile was as reptilian as her bag. "Michel warned her you'd be in over your head...."

Fuck the museum's director!

"....as did other members of the staff, I'm sure," Lily replied. They were probably running a pool on how fast she'd be axed, but she was free of them now. "So good to see you, Gina, but work—"

Gina shook her head. "Knock yourself out on some other canvas, Lily."

"Why?"

"Angela didn't tell you?" Gina clapped her hand to her mouth. Her nails were the color of fresh blood. "I thought you knew!"

Lily silently counted.

Gina smiled sadly. "In exchange for *Schuylerhaugh*, the Rensselaer promised Angela a mint-condition Frederic Church." That artist was Cole's first student, whom some believed had surpassed his master. "She's then going to bundle the Church with a Bierstadt and lend them to the Met for a Renoir."

"*Schuylerhaugh*'s in no condition to travel, Gina."

Gina's look was one of pity. "Nobody expects you to restore it, Lily, Angela just needs you to certify it in a condition report. And surely you have other projects..." She rubbed it in a little more. "As a courtesy to the Kurtz Foundation, Michel and I are more than happy to consult. Our lab is fully staffed. Matt has blossomed under your replacement."

Could she call Matt, would he come? Lily braked right at the edge of Gina's rabbit hole.

"So much for your perfect eye," Gina smirked. "But maybe it's still good for something. Go back to solving crimes, and we'll keep the private consultation on Angela's holdings just between us."

And the entire fucking art world.

Lily gave Gina her bag. "Tempting, but no thanks."

—

Lily turned away from *Schuylerhaugh*. She didn't need Gina to tell her how over her head she was. Was Gina right, were crime scenes all her eye was fit for? But seeing details others missed wasn't just about crime scenes or art. It was about connecting the dots. Frances Glessner Lee had planted tiny clues in her dioramas to make investigators *see*. A fresh espresso in hand, Lily went to her computer to Google her.

The woman who popped up on the screen looked like Agatha Christie's and Winston Churchill's love child. Heavyset, square-faced and jowly, Frances Glessner Lee peered through her wire-rimmed spectacles with a sort of wonderment at the small female mannequin in her hand. She didn't simply dwarf the doll; they were entirely different species. Another photo showed her in a bulky black suit, a peaked hat and a cravat. In yet another she posed proudly in a stiff corsage, flanked by handsome homicide detectives in sharp business suits. The cops' faces shone with adoration and respect. Frances had evidently found her place in an exclusively male field, but what set her on that path? Recalling what Eve had said about the house in which the godmother of crime scene dioramas had been raised, Lily scrolled to it.

The Glessner mansion's granite façade resembled a nineteenth-century jail. Sheltered to near-imprisonment and rigorously tutored at home, Frances had apparently yearned to become a doctor but was forced into a society marriage instead. Interviewed many years later, her son affectionately referred to his mother as FGL and said she should've been born a man. Frances apparently didn't come into her own until she was in her fifties, after she'd divorced and her father had died.

Lily went back to the Glessner manse.

It was a thousand times grander than Dad's bungalow, but its oppressiveness gave her the willies. She could see why Frances' son said their happiest times were living in a rustic cottage after his mother broke free of her parents. Lily returned to a photo of Frances in her studio, her bulldog face furrowed in concentration as she bent over a worktable strewn with tiny furniture and a miniature dressmaker's form. In a strange parody of her parents' obsession with each other and their house, every object in Frances' dioramas worked. From window shades to pencils to door hinges and keys, to a tiny coffee pot with a strainer and grounds... Her obsession was her gift, her real family those beaming homicide cops she'd taught to solve crimes.

Lily used her gift to solve crimes herself.

—

Paul held up a takeout bag from Sushi Den. "For turning your kitchen into a Pollock with my spaghetti the other night."

"You're pulling out all the stops," Lily said, "but it's better than a marriage counselor."

She set the bag on the kitchen counter and grabbed him by his tie.

"Hey—" he said in surprise.

She pulled off the tie and kissed him on the lips. He tasted good, like cloves.

His skin flushed.

She peeled off his suitcoat and pushed him against the counter.

"Wait a second—" But his eyes said something else.

To hell with Louise.

—

Lily caressed the scar that sliced through the curls on Paul's chest.

"Now tell me what's wrong," he said.

She traced the curls down. "Does this feel like something's wrong, Paul?"

Before she could make good on it, he nipped her affectionately on the neck. "I know you too well. What's happening at work?"

She told him about Gina.

"Focus on what you do best, Lily."

"I thought we just did."

Paul laughed. "Seriously, don't let Gina get to you."

He didn't know about Angela's deal with the Met, or how bad a shape the Cole was in. As for what she really did best, Demi's diorama was a cruel reminder of how good it felt to use her eye to solve even a fake murder. "What did you find out about Bliss Byrd?" she asked.

"Her ex is in the clear," Paul replied.

"According to Johnson?" She tried not to make it snide.

"A better source. Hunter Merritt was with Bill in Aspen."

"Hunter…?"

"My new partner." Paul rose. Not many guys pushing fifty looked better in the buff than they did in a suit, even those fancy Italian ones of his. "Speaking of which, the firm's open house is Friday. Cocktails, after work." There went Eve's next diorama. As if reading her mind, he added, "We can swing by DPD on the way."

"To pump poor old Johnson?" she gibed.

"For CT's diorama. You look like you could use a hit of crack." He smiled wickedly. "Shower with me, for old time's sake?" There was more than one way to get her game back. His jacket was on the floor where he'd flung it. He brushed it off and fished a card from the inside pocket. "I'll stick this in your bag."

She rose to join him. "What is it?"

Paul winked. "That realtor."

Chapter Six

Like an iceberg calving from a glacier, a particle of flesh-colored pigment broke off from *Schuylerhaugh*'s sky and left a tiny patch of white. Lily looked down. Salmon buff dust powdered the floor under the easel. The painting was shedding—not just shedding, disintegrating. She stepped back carefully.

Art was mortal, she reminded herself, just looking at and breathing on it hastened its demise. Cave paintings that had endured 40,000 years succumbed to modern pollution; the moment a drawing was completed, it began to fade. *Schuylerhaugh* needed rest and palliative care, not a jaunt to Albany for a cheesy last hurrah. The lab's climate control system suddenly kicked into higher gear, humming like the life support machine it truly was. Except a conservation lab wasn't where art usually went to die.

Lily locked up the lab and left.

The bustle of pedestrians and clot of tourists waiting for tables at the brewpub were comforting reminders that life continued even if a Thomas Cole manor portrait died. It was too early to go home. Should she go shopping and surprise Paul with a real dinner, maybe by candlelight?

Her phone pinged.

Paul. *Clients.*

Scrap dinner.

A drink with Margo? If her old friend wasn't tied up in a high-stakes tax case, she might be up for it. Them as young associates reminded Lily of Demi reaching for Prosser's *Torts*, eager to impress senior partners with knowledge they were too green to know they didn't have. That diorama suddenly felt more real than *Schuylerhaugh*, which brought her back to Angela. Her boss might turn a blind eye to the ethics of shipping an unstable painting to Albany, but Bill Byrd's convenient trip to Aspen the weekend his wife was killed in Highlands would never pass Angela's smell test. Until she knew how and why her friend Bliss had died, she wouldn't let it go.

Lily dug through her purse for her car keys. She still needed groceries, and the kitchen a proper scrubbing. Highlands was across I-25, opposite from home.

Ping. Paul again. *Realtor?*

She put her phone in her bag and tossed it on the passenger seat. Three minutes later, she was crossing the highway for the northwest side of town.

—

The Italian immigrants who'd built Highlands would never recognize it now. Gone were the stone yards whose cement angels had adorned mausoleums, and the spaghetti-and-meatball joints where what passed for Denver's mafia had supped. Gentrification marched on. The Latino restaurants and edgy co-op galleries that muscled out the mafia had fled to suburbs where the rent was cheaper. Now there was an artisan bread company, a high-end consignment store, and a coffee shop on every corner.

Lily smelled what was left of Bliss Byrd's house before she saw it. Four days had passed since the explosion, but an acrid odor hung in the air and yellow crime scene tape festooned the lawn. Adam had been wrong; the tiny house hadn't been parked out back, nor did it have wheels. Its rubble was heaped between an imposing Queen Anne with a turret and scalloped shingles and a Tiffany blue *For Sale* sign with a black logo.

"Can I help you?" A neighbor with a watering hose was frowning at her. Lily didn't blame him; he was probably sick of looky-loos, and she had no official business or right to intrude.

"I knew Bliss," she said.

He squinted over his bifocals. He looked to be in his fifties, older than the Gen Xers flocking to this side of town. "A client?"

"Not exactly."

"Bill will never sell it now," he said bitterly. He trained his hose on a new patch of grass. His own house was a trim craftsman bungalow with a big front porch. What was it like to stare every day at Bliss' glorified dollhouse?

"I'm sure—" she began sympathetically.

He needed no further invitation to spill. "I filed the code complaint. She could've put that damn thing in the garage." A three-car detached one sat at the end of the driveway that ran behind the Queen Anne. He momentarily brightened. "That realtor will sure take a hit. She was here today, trying to put a happy face on the mess."

Lily glanced at the *For Sale* sign. The logo said TR Realty. A handsome ginger cat sidled over, and she knelt to pet him. He'd lost his whiskers and his tail was singed. He rubbed against the neighbor's legs; despite ratting Bliss out, maybe the guy wasn't so bad.

A woman in capris emerged from the bungalow and scratched the cat behind his ears. "Thank God Mickey escaped," she told Lily. "We're taking him in."

"Carole…" the man warned.

"Bill doesn't want him?" Lily asked.

Carole rolled her eyes in the direction of the *For Sale* sign. "He's got Trudi Rood."

"Bill was a saint till his wife got into that decluttering crap," the man said. "Spark Bliss—and how!"

"Howard!"

"That propane-powered minifridge was just waiting to blow, Carole—"

Maybe it was an accident.

"—tried to buy her out so he could tear the damn thing down. Now his lawn's a smoldering mess, he's got a realtor who doesn't know her ass from her elbow, and all that's left of Bliss is a pair of gardening boots with the soles fused to—"

"Howard!"

Gardening boots? Bliss must have tried to get out.

The Byrds' garage opened. A black SUV slowly backed down the driveway.

"Look who's here," Carole said.

"Doesn't propane stink?" Lily asked Howard.

He nodded. "Like a skunk."

The SUV coasted towards them. The driver started to wave.

"You nailed that door shut, Bill!" Carole shouted.

"Carole!" Howard said.

"The fireman said so!" she yelled.

Bill flipped Carole off.

"They have the door!" she cried.

The SUV's wheels screeched as it turned onto the street.

"Him and that damned realtor," Carole muttered.

Lily opened her purse and found Paul's card.

Tiffany blue. TR Realty was Trudi Rood.

Chapter Seven

In bed that night with a bowl of cornflakes and her laptop, Lily Googled Trudi Rood.

TR's signage could afford to be classy and brash; Trudi's tentacles were everywhere. Just this year she'd racked up two dozen million-dollar-plus sales and been engaged as exclusive agent for units in a revamped industrial complex in trendy RiNo. The photo on her website showed a stately blonde with sapphire eyes and impressive teeth.

Lily dialed the number on the Tiffany blue card.

On the go, a perky voice answered. *Call you back!*

She returned to her computer.

Bliss Byrd was easy to find, too—as an executive coach. On LinkedIn, her client roster included Coca-Cola and AT&T, and the accompanying testimonials had evaded HR's red pen to come across as surprisingly personal and warm. Bliss' stamp-sized photo showed a redhead in a black blazer with her hair tightly pulled back and a smile that showed no teeth. Angela had said she'd reinvented herself, but how did Bliss go from consulting in Fortune 500 boardrooms to living in a tiny house?

Lily Googled Bliss Byrd + decluttering.

Nothing.

Bliss Byrd + tiny house. News items about the explosion, no obit.

Paul pinged. *Don't wait up.* Tomorrow night she'd finally meet those new partners of his. Her cell rang, but she ignored it; Dad never called this late. Bliss' new gig must be on the web. Her neighbor Howard had used a funny expression… She typed in Spark Bliss + Bill Byrd.

A YouTube video: *Spark Bliss with Bliss Byrd!*

Lily clicked the arrow.

The screen filled with a busty gal with flowing red hair and an appealing gap in her front teeth: Bliss Byrd, reincarnated as Earth Mother. "Today you," Bliss promised, "tomorrow the world." Birds chirped and cheery pots of geraniums flanked her red door. Bliss flung her arms out. "Welcome to my world!" The camera panned to a ginger tomcat wending between her legs. Bliss winked. "Miko." Had that red door been nailed shut?

Bliss and Miko led Lily through it.

"Morning's my favorite time," Bliss confided on the screen. "I start with tea brewed from chamomile from my own garden." She pointed to the water heater in her kitchenette. "At bedtime I re-boil it." Miko jumped up on the counter and sniffed at a colander filled with beets, an onion and a bunch of carrots. "I make soup with the peelings—leftovers are delicious! Nothing goes to waste."

Lily's phone pinged again, but the video was hypnotic.

Bliss wagged her finger playfully. "Keep only things that spark bliss," she advised, "not books you've outgrown or paintings that take up too much space." Her walls were bare—no art. "How liberating to throw it all away!"

Bliss Byrd had curated her life, but could you curate bliss?

She led the viewer to a nook with a drop-down desk and a laptop. "How did we live before Zoom?" she lamented. A three-in-one printer perched atop a paper shredder. Lily giggled. Did Bliss cook dinner with the shreddings, or stuff them into her meditation pillow? But silly as it might be, to her this little place had been *home.*

Bliss climbed a carpeted ladder to a sleeping loft, with Miko at her heels. They seemed inseparable; if she were indeed murdered, did the killer use him as bait? Lily pictured Bliss banging at that red door, frantic to find him. "—all sparks Bliss," she was saying, "and gratitude. For Miko, you—even my divorce. My new wellness partner is helping me design a product line—"

The phone rang again. Paul... Dad? Lily muted the video and answered it. But her mind was still on Bliss. Despite her bounteous aura, there was something wary in her eyes. If it wasn't her husband, who hated her enough to kill her? And Miko—

"Lily Sparks?" the woman on the phone said.

"Yes?"

"Trudi Rood." The realtor.

Lily refocused. "I saw your sign. That Queen Anne in Highlands?"

Trudi hesitated. "The big house—of course. Great listing, temporarily off the market. The owner's doing a couple of tweaks, but we'd better move fast because Denver's red hot. I just flipped a place that sold for two-hundred grand more than last year. What exactly are you looking for?"

"Um... Two baths and a den."

Trudi laughed easily. "That can be arranged. Now tell me about you."

On screen, Bliss Byrd and her cat soundlessly snipped herbs from a pot by the door. The killer didn't have to know her personally to use Miko as bait. He just needed YouTube.

Chapter Eight

The tiny conservatory reminded Lily of a glass-domed jewelry box. Beneath the dome, intricate objects in gemstone colors were arrayed on a maze of mini-benches. At the center of the maze a body—a man, from his build and the remains of his head—lay face up. Red mist dappled a glass wall.

"Shotgun to the kisser," Johnson said. "Old-style."

"There is something *classic* about it," Paul agreed.

"Colonel Mustard, meet Miz Scarlet!" a detective cried.

Eve Castle waited for the hoots to die. The cops were antsy for the weekend. Some looked forward to a Friday night beer, others were gearing up for shootings and domestic violence calls. Johnson stifled a yawn as Lily slowly circled the diorama.

Like a velvet tray with compartments for earrings, the benches showcased a stunning display of bonsai. A graceful red leaf maple, a stand of cypress, a juniper whose trunk twisted like a crane. The man lay at the base of a tall pedestal.

"Tell me about Glenn," Eve asked.

The beetle-browed rookie's ID tag said Bowles. "Widowed

proctologist—" he began.

"—urologist!" Johnson sighed. "Someday you'll know the difference, kid."

"—and bonsai master," Bowles continued reading from the script. "Fifty percent art, fifty percent science, fifty percent Zen."

"Golf," Johnson muttered.

Paul chuckled.

"Your score, or the humblebrag?" an older cop asked Johnson. "Ever notice how golfers—"

Eve had come around the diorama to stand at Lily's shoulder. "What does Glenn's hobby tell us?" she asked softly.

"It wasn't a hobby," Lily replied, "it was art." Each bonsai was showcased like a precious stone. "Did he cultivate them?"

Eve nodded. "Glenn recently took top prize in Kyoto for a grove of nine junipers, one for each core competency in his surgical subspecialty." She smiled inscrutably. "A bonsai is never completed." And some dioramas weren't meant to be solved. "Who saw him last?" she asked the detectives.

"Another retired doc." Johnson squinted at the script. "Every Thursday night they had dinner and a bottle of red. When Glenn didn't answer the phone later, his pal went over to check."

"Hmm," Eve said at Lily's elbow. "What's missing in plain sight?"

Bonsai... prize... blood. Lily rounded the conservatory again. Glenn's specimens weren't genetic dwarves; bonsai miniaturized nature by stunting roots and shoots. This attack was equally controlled and brutal.

"Those docs had a history," Bowles mused.

"Lover's quarrel explains the rage," Johnson said.

From across the diorama, Lily looked at Eve. "Retired urologist shooting a colleague in the face? Not that Glenn *was* shot."

The cops stopped shuffling.

Eve blinked. "Continue."

"Firing a shotgun in a conservatory is like exploding a bomb in a bell jar," Lily explained. "The bonsai would be covered with skull fragments and blood. I'd look for a tool sharp enough to penetrate bone and produce that spray."

Bowles and the other cops were rapt.

"What's missing in plain sight?" Lily continued. "Glenn's juniper grove, the prize-winning bonsai which belongs on that pedestal."

Paul shook his head in admiration, and Johnson whistled through his teeth.

Eve smiled tightly. "Who killed him?"

Lily grinned. "Ask the master Glenn beat for that prize."

Chapter Nine

Paul swiped his ID card across the elevator pad in his LoDo boutique firm's reincarnation of brick, metal and glass. "Some show back there tonight."

"Eve bet me brunch." Lily hadn't been to a law firm bash in years but pumped from gobsmacking Johnson again and going 2-0 with Eve Castle, she found herself looking forward to this one. Maybe she'd meet the guy who represented Bill Byrd. "Speaking of tiny crime scenes, did you know Bliss' door was nailed shut?"

"Bliss?" Paul asked as the elevator silently arrived.

"Angela's friend—Hunter Merritt's client's ex."

"Who told you about the door?" Paul asked as they got in.

"A neighbor."

He turned. "Don't tell me you—"

The elevator opened onto a reception area with an onyx desk, a steel wall etched with the firm's initials, and cocktails in full swing. Casual Friday evidently meant Italian loafers instead of Oxfords, and dress shirts with the top button undone. Gone were nylons and the little blue suit; flirty dresses showed off toned arms and bare legs. The glass-walled conference room had an elaborate spread of hors d'oeuvres, but the crowd was thickest at a table across the floor. Paul yanked off his tie and stuffed it in his pocket. "I'll grab us a beer." He probably had a dozen craft ales to choose from.

Lily watched him move through the throng. Despite his crack about white-collar crime paying too well, Paul seemed all too at home here. Before he could take two steps, he was intercepted by a slim man in a suit two shades darker than his silver hair. Another fellow squeezed his shoulder and introduced him to someone else. Paul looked back at her with a helpless shrug; intros and craft ale would have to wait.

A black-haired man at the far wall saluted Lily with his highball. She turned and adjusted the neckline of her blouse. She'd gone straight from the lab to DPD; Paul should have told her to wear a dress. Across the way an older woman in a tight black sheath was staring at the man with the highball. Catching his eye, she gestured impatiently. He turned away. A girl in a flirty dress was clinging to Paul's arm. This time he didn't look back. Where were the female partners and wives?

"Some shindig." In khakis and a polo shirt, Adam Castle looked as out of place as Lily felt.

"You mean meat market," she replied.

He chuckled. "Not quite what I pictured when Paul said open house, but it's kind of him to show me around."

"Where's Eve?"

"Mopping up at DPD. She'll be here later."

The black-haired man had snagged two pints of lager. The sheath-clad cougar was determinedly making her way towards him. Lily turned back to Adam. "I've been meaning to ask…"

"That prize-winning bonsai grove?" He winked. "Eve missed it, but you nailed it."

"The cat."

"Cat?" His wire-rims flashed.

"Demi's calico," Lily said.

"Oh! The hobby market's exploding with miniaturists. An incredible

German woman hand paints—"

"Whose idea was it?" she asked.

Adam blushed. "I always wanted a pet, but Eve hates cats and dogs."

Across the room, Paul was signaling the bartender.

Adam squeezed her elbow. "I'll go thank him myself."

The crowd grew noisier. Adam joined Paul, who introduced him to the partner in the sharkskin suit. Having dodged the woman in the sheath, the black-haired man was coming Lily's way. Paul interrupted him. She speed-scanned the layout. Past the conference room was a corridor. She quickly turned down it.

The first office was brightly lit. Artsy posters hung on the wall, and the chairs were stacked with files. Associates never slept. In the second, the computer was on screensaver—a young partner would be returning soon. Hearing footsteps behind her, Lily ducked into the corner office. Bold abstract painting, granite desk and leather couch—

The black-haired man stood between her and the door, holding the two lagers. "You look like you could use a drink," he said.

"I was looking for the ladies room," she replied.

He grinned. "I won't tell. Especially since this office is mine."

Lily accepted the lager.

He leaned against his desk and smiled at her quizzically. He was even better-looking up close, and not the least drunk. Served Paul right. "You're not a lawyer," he said, sipping his drink. "How am I doing?"

Strike one.

"Or a colleague's wife," he continued. "I would've seen you before."

Lily nodded noncommittally. After the diorama, it was fun watching someone else make the moves. And the lager was cold and smooth.

"Or a client," he concluded.

"Why not?" she asked.

He grinned. "Whoever brought you would be showing you off."

She should end this, but the edgy abstract grabbed her eye. She'd seen that burst of indigo in the upper left corner somewhere before. "Nice painting. Are you a collector?"

"Three more at my penthouse." He winced at the corny line. "I saw you eyeing the hors d'oeuvres. How about a steak?"

"I—" she began.

Paul stood in the doorway with Adam.

"Hunter," Paul said tightly. Bill Byrd's lawyer.

Hunter straightened. "Hey, Paul. Let me introduce you to—"

"Lily Sparks." With one smooth step, Paul put his arm around her waist.

Hunter smiled ruefully. "Should've known the most beautiful gal in the room was with you, but I thought you were living out of a suitcase at your hotel."

Paul had been staying with her for a month. What else didn't he tell his new partners? Adam was watching all three of them curiously.

"Guess you won't be looking for a fancy bachelor pad after all," Hunter continued. Paul's grip on her waist tightened. "Trudi'll be disappointed. She closed on my penthouse." He winked at Lily. "My offer still stands."

She pivoted to the abstract. "Did Trudi introduce you to the artist, too?"

"His patron," Hunter said. "Trudi—"

"We have an appointment with her," Paul interrupted.

Hunter set down his lager. "So you think you know what you want?" he asked Lily with an insinuating grin. "Maybe after another drink—"

"We'll take a raincheck," Paul said.

———

Eve hadn't shown, so they dropped Adam at his parking lot. Lily watched him drive off in a sporty pickup. "You sure Bill Byrd was in Aspen last weekend?" she asked Paul.

He flung his jacket in the backseat. "Stay out of it, Lily."

"Too late. You promised Angela—"

"Johnson's already interviewed Bliss Byrd's neighbors," he said.

"Yeah?" Lily replied. "Ask him about her door."

Chapter Ten

As Lily braked for joggers crossing the road from Cheesman's gravel path, birds chirped and the morning was spanking new. Far too new to spend Saturday watching *Schuylerhaugh* shed. She'd bought a little time with Angela, and Paul was in D.C. till Tuesday. But his dismissal of Bliss Byrd's nailed door last night still rankled, and Hunter Merritt thinking Paul was in the market for a bachelor pad ticked her off. Him expecting her to go house-hunting with Trudi Rood while he gadded about with Hunter was icing on the cake. Paul might not care where they lived, but she did. Their new house would be on a park. Which one? The intersection cleared, and she abruptly made a U-turn to head in the opposite direction of the lab.

Cherry Creek was an overbuilt construction zone.

Congress Park's old bungalows were like Dad's; just driving past gave her hives.

Before she knew it, the Prius was circling Cranmer Park. Barren and frisbee-shaped, the tilted swathe of yellow grass was mainly used as a middle-school soccer field. But the houses on the east side were on higher ground and had spectacular views of the Front Range. As if to underscore the privilege of ownership, those houses were unfenced, and this morning the price for that privilege was dog-walkers and kids in school jerseys trampling the grass that grew right to the door of a familiar Modernist mansion with a cantilevered roof.

Bruce Kemp's house.

House? Elena had scoffed three months ago, when they'd been there at a soirée. *You mean gas station. No wonder he lives alone.*

Lily circled the park and braked. Now she saw that the dogs and people weren't just strays from the soccer field; cops were cordoning off Bruce's house. Coasting past, through floor-to-ceiling windows she saw men milling around a tent inside. One plainclothes guy scraped something off the interior of a window.

This was a crime scene.

Bruce Kemp must be dead.

Lily drove around back and parked behind a phalanx of police vehicles. A vintage Mercedes convertible with cherry upholstery and canvas top sat in Bruce's carport.

Not even a garage, Elena had sniffed.

As Lily crunched across the graveled yard, she ran through what she knew about Bruce Kemp.

Divorced.

Green entrepreneur and art collector.

He'd made a killing off of "safe" fracking technology and invested it in local artists. For the soirée, his house had been lit like a department store window. The uninvited could look but not touch. A killer had evidently done both. The back of Bruce's house was curtained.

Even narcissists have limits, Elena had said.

Now a uniformed cop stood at the back door. "No trespassing, ma'am," he said politely.

"I knew Bruce." She tried to see past him.

He blocked her view. "No reporters."

She gestured at her sneakers and jeans. "Do I look like a reporter?" His brows beetled—the rookie at yesterday's diorama. She glanced at his

ID tag. "Bowles, right? What's hiding in plain sight?"

The rookie's face lit. "Miss… Sparks?"

She winked. "Is Johnson in charge?" The young cop glanced behind him. "No need to bother him, Bowles. Who found Bruce?"

"You'll love this." Bowles lowered his voice discreetly. "Couple of dog-walkers thought the blood spatter on the wall was a painting! His housekeeper called it in." A distraught woman stood with Johnson by the tent. Lily edged past Bowles for a closer look.

For the soirée, canvases had been mounted on movable walls. Now Bruce's ground floor was wide open. The tent stood in a corner, and skull and brain tissue were plastered on the textured wall behind it. Johnson glanced up. Seeing Lily, his eyes widened in disbelief.

"Who saw Bruce last?" she quickly asked Bowles.

"An artist," he said. "Drinks—"

Johnson was coming fast.

"Gunshot?" she asked Bowles.

"To the head."

"What the hell are you doing here!" Johnson demanded.

"I knew Bruce," she tried.

"Yeah, you and every goddamn—" He gave Bowles a dirty look and grabbed Lily by the elbow. She took one last look. Bruce's loafered foot protruded from the tent. Blood had sprayed not just the wall behind the tent, but the soaring window facing the park. The killer had cornered Bruce Kemp between the wall and that window. Was it to display his own work?

Chapter Eleven

En route to the lab, Lily replayed Bruce Kemp's soirée.

The guests had been Denver's high-end art crowd: museum director Michel Roland and upper-level staff, gallerists, and patrons. The new class of patrons wanted to look poor, but artists truly were; Lily could always spot them by their keen eyes, shaggy hair, and shabby wardrobes. Bruce's guest of honor had enormous glasses, pants falling down, a cream jacket with clownish lapels he must've borrowed from his dad—and a shy sweet smile, like he couldn't believe how lucky he was to hold a paintbrush. *It's how I keep from dying*, she'd heard him say. Dodging Gina, she and Elena had snagged flutes of champagne.

"So talented," Elena sighed.

A maze of movable walls led guests to a massive abstract with an enormous indigo burst tailing down like a comet. The labyrinth made the experience curiously intimate, and with the crowd it was impossible to see everyone. But looking back on it now, something was familiar …

Lily refocused on the artist.

The museum had been considering mounting a show, or at least acquiring one of his paintings. Red-dotted labels had said most were sold. The rest ran in the low five figures. Bruce watched intently from a corner, alternating between hearty handshakes for patrons and knowing grins for collectors. "Chum for chumps," Elena murmured. "Poor kid."

"Bruce?" Lily had asked.

"The artist." An assistant affixed another red dot to a label. "He started out with smaller canvases, but Bruce pushed him to scale up. From the very beginning, that indigo comet was his motif."

"Well, he can buy a jacket that fits him now," Lily said, "and the museum—" Gina waved from the hors d'oeuvres. The hedge funder with her was in jeans and a sport coat, the kind of man who thrived on tax dodges and risk—Gina offered both. But Elena was looking askance at Bruce. "What've you got against him?" Lily had asked.

"Pump-and-dump," Elena had said. "Bruce flips paintings to run up prices at auction. Before the artist knows what hit, he's overpriced and his work is toast. Forget that museum show." She'd gestured sadly to the kid in the clown coat. "Crumbs now, bupkis later. Like that comet tailing down …"

—

Gina was waiting outside the lab with a shopping bag from the gourmet olive oil store down the block. Pulling to the curb, Lily eyed her with feigned delight. "Gina! You shouldn't have…"

Gina clutched the bag to her bony chest. "Shouldn't what?"

"Brave a trip to this end of LoDo on Saturday with a lab-warming gift."

Tourists in shorts and sunglasses jostled Gina in her wedged espadrilles, pushing her into the path of a couple with a stroller laden with a toddler and produce from the Union Station farmers' market. She caught her balance and lowered her bag. As she edged closer to the Prius, Lily considered rolling up her window, but Gina put her hand on the sill and smiled at Lily like a snake. "Just thought I'd—"—*check out what fucking bad shape Schuylerhaugh's in so I can tell*—"—share some news."

"You're leaving DAM?" Lily asked.

"What? No!" Gina's bag almost hit the cement.

"Careful with that vinegar," Lily said. "Just a rumor, I guess. Well, say hi to Michel—"

Gina set her bag carefully on the sidewalk. Arms crossed, she planted her espadrilles firmly between the Prius and the lab. A loud group of twenty-somethings exited the corner café for the brewpub across the street. Between mojitos at brunch and dead drunk at midnight, LoDo on a weekend was an all-day happy hour. She waited for the hubbub to subside, then spoke with a sotto voce gravity. "Bruce Kemp was murdered."

"Wow! When?"

"Last night. He just lost a big green-energy contract." Gina could barely conceal her glee; had that hedge funder she'd been dating shorted Bruce's stock? "And his soirée was a bust."

"Sure sold lots of paintings…"

"Bombed at auction, flooding the secondary market." Gina leaned on the door, suffusing the smell of sunbaked garbage in the gutter with her cloying scent. "A hunky lawyer bought three. I bet he's pissed."

Hunter Merritt? Lily had to call Paul, but not with Gina watching. What was Gina really here for, a peek at Angela's hidden trove? She and Michel wouldn't stop until the museum got its hands on it. Lily revved the Prius to make noise.

Gina leaned in the window. "Of course, those paintings may be worth something now. Nothing like murder to give a painting cachet."

Lily turned up the AC and angled the vent at her.

Gina seemed not to notice. "Speaking of cachet, I saw *Schuylerhaugh* in *Fine Arts Connoisseur*. It's the centerpiece of the Rensselaer's show. Can I use your loo?"

You just did. "So sorry, Gina! I don't normally work Saturdays, but I stopped to see if the plumber came. These fancy Japanese bidets… But there's a Subway down the street. Want a lift?"

Gina reared back.

Lily slowly circled the block. She lost her parking spot, but it was worth it.

Gina was gone.

—

As Lily unlocked the lab, her cell rang. Not Angela—an unidentified number

"Lily?" It was Eve Castle. "Angela gave me your number. Am I bothering you at work?"

"Not at all!"

"I owe you brunch," Eve said. "You like mimosas?"

"And screwdrivers."

Eve laughed. "That kind of day, eh? If you can wait till tomorrow, I'll bring the vodka."

A bottomless screwdriver might do the trick. If she got drunk enough, she could pitch a quart of vodka and orange juice at *Schuylerhaugh* and watch it dissolve.

"Delphine's tomorrow at eleven," Eve said. "We won't talk crime or art."

"Sold."

Chapter Twelve

That evening, Lily Googled Bruce Kemp.

Denver native, old-line Country Club. East Coast prep school, School of Mines—a top engineering school—Wharton MBA and stint at Lazard. Then The Cactus Club, a younger hand replacing arthritic ones still clutching the local levers of power. Did he meet Hunter there? She didn't remember Hunter being at the soirée…. She went back to Bruce.

Married twice, divorced, no kids—no surprise. A family trust owned the house on Cranmer Park, which explained the gas-station design and why it looked like nobody actually lived there. Closing her eyes, Lily visualized it again. Not the crime scene or the soirée, but from inside a glass house looking out. Either you wanted people to look in, or you had nothing to hide. Everyone had secrets—what was Bruce's? And there was another thing, too.

Take her condo's balcony doors. With the lights off and in the black of night, she and Paul could wander around nude. Lights on, the glass mirrored their mundane domesticity. But sometimes alone at night, staring out of her own floor-to-ceiling glass, the vast empty space staring back wasn't so friendly. It swallowed her. The dioramas were just the opposite; they confined brutality and gore to a tiny space. After growing up in a granite mausoleum, did that compact confinement attract Frances Glessner Lee too?

Lily fixed herself a decaf. It was late, but she speed-dialed Paul. No answer. Where was he staying in D.C.? Four Seasons. Natch—a pool. Courtesy of the bank president, back on an expense account. She called the hotel.

"Paul Reilly?" a cultured female voice said. "I'll check..."

At least he'd checked in—Lily stopped herself. What had she been thinking, he and Hunter were off on a toot?

"...Mr. Reilly is not answering..."

Out to dinner—at 11:00 p.m. in D.C.?

"... can I take a message?"

Now Lily felt foolish. Not just foolish, but regretting she'd called. Paul would ask what was going on with *Schuylerhaugh*, and say she was using Bruce Kemp's murder—*mackerel to a seal, hit of crack!*—to avoid the lab and finding them a house. But the dioramas had sucked her in.

"Miss?" the woman asked.

"No message, thanks."

Lily gave Jack some kibble and a belly rub, then stared out her balcony door. Not everyone cared about privacy. Maybe Bruce was an exhibitionist, he wanted to force the world to see him and his paintings in all their glory. Did the wrong person look? Jack jumped up on the couch. She thought of Bliss Byrd—and Miko. Doors nailed shut and windows that didn't open. Bruce collected art, Glenn cultivated bonsai.... She texted Paul. *Call b4 bed.*

No response.

What did home mean to Bliss and Bruce? They couldn't have grown up in houses that were tiny or made of glass.

Ping. From Angela. *Cole call?*

That ended her reverie with a thud. Delivering Bliss Byrd's killer to Angela on a slab wouldn't make up for *Schuylerhaugh*. She knew what Angela would do—and Gina. Fudge the condition report. Lard it with enough caveats to shift the risk to the Rensselaer. Even pretend the painting wasn't in such bad shape. Hell—maybe it'd survive the trip to Albany. And if it didn't, who cared? Not Benjy Schuyler, free at last from having to salute it. He'd still deliver the keynote.

She texted Paul again. No reply.

She gave Jack another treat. "We're going to start a real life with Paul."

Jack crunched.

"We're buying a house," she told him.

He looked up for more treats.

"We have to pay our way. *Schuylerhaugh* isn't worth our job."

If she knew Angela, the pressure to fudge the condition report would only mount. But what about her responsibility to the artist, Thomas Cole? Young and broke, he'd painted *Schuylerhaugh* for room and board. The manor portrait was no Hudson River School masterpiece, but it had survived for two hundred years. Which would fuck up her life more: refusing to sign a bullshit condition report or giving that painting a one-way first-class ticket to its doom? And did Cole himself contemplate the mortality of his work? Wondering what that might have meant to him, she started scrolling her laptop. At a news story on renovations to his 1800's homestead in Catskill, New York, she paused.

Hand-painted friezes had been found under old layers of paint in Cole's pantry and parlor. That Cole painted directly onto his own walls wasn't so surprising; as a lad in Lancashire, England, he'd apprenticed to a designer of calico prints, and when his family emigrated to America his father had manufactured wallpaper. Or did he paint the friezes because he couldn't resist the impulse to extend his art? *It's how I keep from dying,* said that skinny artist with the clownish lapels at Bruce Kemp's soirée.

If Cole was driven to paint on his very walls, and a young artist centuries later felt his art stood between him and death, how did a painter feel about a patron like Bruce dumping his works onto the secondary market? And Cole's friezes reminded Lily of something Adam Castle had said: *Every house had a secret.*

The Kurtz Castle's secret was the alcove behind the library; like Cole's friezes, the alcove had been covered over, first in celadon-and-gold, now in a grass print. The secret room had been replicated in Angela's baby dollhouse. If a room could be hidden in a house, could a real house—

Riiiing. Her cell.

"What's up?" Paul said. The clank of dishes in his background made it sound like he was calling from a restaurant. He'd have a field day with the idea of real houses hiding in dioramas, or a mousy artist killing his patron.

"Still holding hands?" she replied brightly.

"With the client? Hunter's babysitting him."

"Hunter?" If he bought his abstracts at Bruce's soirée and their value had tanked, he was a better candidate for Bruce's killer than the artist who'd painted them. "Tell him we'll take him up on his offer."

Paul moved to a quieter corner. "What offer?"

"To visit his condo."

"*I* wasn't invited," he said sharply.

She tried to make it sound like fun. "That abstract in his office—I just love the artist!"

Kitchen sounds, waiters on a break.

"What's going on, Lily?" Paul finally said.

"I... ran into Johnson today."

Paul chuckled grimly. "At a cop dive, or a crime scene?"

"Crime scene. He threw me out." She told him about Bruce being murdered, and that she thought Hunter Merritt might have bought his abstracts at Bruce's soirée. She could hear Paul shake his head. "What did Johnson say about Bliss' door?"

"It blew up with the house, Lily."

"But the neighbors—"

Paul sighed. "In case you haven't noticed, neighbors are full of shit."

Bill Byrd's neighbor Carole certainly had it in for him. "But what if Hunter and Bruce—"

"Why do you suddenly care?" Paul demanded.

"Too many coincidences, Paul! First Bill Byrd's ex, now Bruce Kemp..."

He laughed dismissively. "Their only connection is a well-connected lawyer. And speaking of connections, did you make an appointment with that realtor?"

"Tuesday." Trudi had better be available. "And you're coming too, Paul."

Chapter Thirteen

Built by a soap baron and reincarnated as a Mexican restaurant, Delphine's in Highlands now offered Cajun and Creole food. This Sunday, Eve waited with a crowd of people on the shady porch. She and Lily exchanged a hug.

"Am I late?" Lily asked.

"They'll text us." Eve gave a friendly nod to a young couple behind them. "Married or dating?" she whispered to Lily. "No fair peeking at hands."

The girl had a ring, the boy didn't. She also had a slightly frantic look, like something more important was waiting at home. What did young parents call themselves these days? "Engaged," Lily said.

Eve nodded. "And?"

The boy looked nervous. "He owes her one."

"Meaning?"

"It's their anniversary," Lily said. "He owes her for being the parent while they both work."

Ping. Their table was ready. The waiter led them to a courtyard with wrought iron furniture and pots of pansies.

"Adam made me promise to order beignets," Eve confided. "It's his favorite spot."

The beignets arrived hot and heaped with powdered sugar. Lily's mimosa came in a mason jar garnished with lime; Eve's Bloody Mary had a pickle. The neighboring table vacated and the waiter seated the young couple.

"Oh, goody," Eve said, and moved her chair next to Lily's for a better view. "Not as much fun as a bar, but domestic scenes are always fertile ground."

The boy reached for the girl's hand; she stared at her phone. "Checking the sitter," Lily guessed. "They have a starter dog at home, too."

Eve winced. "Golden lab."

This was loads more fun than Lily's own lab. They toasted the couple.

"How'd you meet Paul?" Eve asked.

"Opposite sides of a case."

Eve stopped watching the other table.

"My firm represented Elena's gallery," Lily explained. "The Feds charged her with selling a looted watercolor, and he was on the FBI's Art Theft Team."

"Who won?" Eve asked.

"Elena."

"And you became a paintings conservator!" They clicked jars and drank. "How did you meet Angela?"

"Paul came back to Denver later, when her father was murdered." Lily spared Eve the gory details of George Kurtz's death and Paul facing the killer down in that filthy shed. Watching the young couple sip chai at the other table, she wondered what Eve made of her and Paul. "How did you and Adam meet?"

Eve ordered a second round of drinks. "I was doing a Masters in Psych at Tulane under Frank Gould."

"Frank…?"

"Forensic guru. I wanted to counsel abused kids."

"And did you?" Lily asked.

Eve sighed. "It's how I got into dollhouses professionally. Enacting family dramas on a tiny stage lets kids write their own scripts. The wonder is more adults don't..." She frowned. "Uh-oh."

Lily glanced over at the next table. The boy's leg jiggled, and the girl's feet now pointed away from his. She turned back to Eve. "Why'd you stop working with abused kids?"

"The dolls."

"Dolls?" Lily pictured Frances Glessner Lee knitting stockings with straight pins.

Eve nodded sadly. "Therapy ones are more realistic now, but back then they scared my patients. Weird skin tones, scowling faces ..." But hadn't that baby doll in Angela's wall been scary precisely because it was so lifelike? "The kids' reactions made me curious about what drove their offenders," she continued, "so I went back to Frank for a PhD in Forensic Psychology in Oregon. Dioramas are definitely more my speed." She laughed ruefully. "It's a helluva lot easier when the dolls are dead."

The waiter opened an umbrella to shield them from the sun. With the young couple now out of view, Eve and Lily turned to their food.

"How did Adam feel about your going back to school?" Lily asked.

"He'd landed that luxury tower in Miami." Eve made it sound like the Pritzker Prize was no big deal, but a note of self-doubt had crept into her voice. "The timing was crap, titanium doubled the cost, and buyers started unloading units. His last couple of D.C. commissions weren't even built." She stared at her drink. "And I was questioning whether I was doing him or those abused kids any good at all."

"And Castle Training—"

"—didn't just save our marriage." Eve tossed down her Bloody Mary. "It brought me back to myself. But we promised not to talk crime. Tell me what you and Paul want."

"Want?"

She patted Lily's hand. "Adam says you're buying a house."

"We just started looking."

"For a storybook cottage?" Eve asked.

Lily shook her head empathically. "I'm not the white picket fence type."

Eve looked up. "Do I detect a... distaste for ivy?"

"Virginia Creeper." And small dark rooms.

"The stuff of nightmares!" Eve smiled sympathetically. "But no space is benign or malign, Lily. Experience makes it so."

Tell that to Demi—or Bliss Byrd. And what about Glenn in his conservatory, or Bruce Kemp in his glass house? Human or dolls, they were all killed at home. Were the victims the targets, or was it something about their houses? Lily laughed to herself. Better not tell that to Paul, or let Eve talk her into a third pint of mimosas.

"Lily, dear?" Eve said.

Crime scenes and dioramas tumbled through Lily's head. Something darker burbled up—a memory of being in bed at night in her old room at Dad's bungalow. After Mom died, she'd press her ear to the wall, yearning to hear their fights again—anything to show she was still alive. Mom's scent had lingered for a while but soon that vanished too. Anger would have been better than the gaping void her death had left, or Dad's halting step as he trod the hallway to the kitchen where he sat every night with his head in his hands. And what had he given her to make up for what he took? Nothing but the perfect-eye game...

"Lily?" Eve said.

She looked up with a start. Dad's bungalow had always been home, why did it suddenly creep her out now? Maybe it was the foliage that threatened to swallow *Schuylerhaugh*, or Frances Glessner Lee's cheery granite crypt. Or the crab Benedict, too rich after those beignets and these all-too-welcome distractions from work. Lily pushed away her plate. Paul was right. Instead of getting sloshed with Eve and trying to solve imaginary murders by looking for connections that didn't exist, she should get her own houses in order. She owed Trudi a call to make sure she had Tuesday open.

The waiter passed by with oyster po' boys for the next table. The girl abruptly stood, almost knocking over the waiter and their umbrella. The boy threw down some cash. Hand in hand they left. "That baby at home," Lily guessed.

Eve nodded. "Call it a draw. But there's one more diorama...."

"When?"

"Tuesday." Eve swirled her ice. "Winner buys cocktails?"

"Deal. What's the scene?"

"A high rise." Eve chuckled. "Now let's talk about your house. You have a realtor?"

"Trudi Rood."

"I know Trudi!" Eve exclaimed. Who didn't? Bill Byrd, Hunter Merritt... She gave a little frown. "She sold us our place—why, we should have you and Paul over for dinner, just the four of us." Not Angela—did Eve somehow intuit she was ducking her? "We've moved around so much we don't know anybody here in Denver. Michel and his gal Friday got us into a private event or two, but it's tough making new friends. You're so lucky to have Angela."

Reminded of the lab, Lily stooped for her purse.

Eve seized her arm. "Spaces aren't good or evil, Lily."

The bungalow. "So you said."

Eve converted the squeeze to a pat. "And Frank taught me something else."

"What?" Lily asked.

"Storybook cottages never are."

Chapter Fourteen

Scrubbing the last speck of tomato sauce from her stove's backsplash that evening, Lily vowed their new kitchen range would be on an island. As she tackled the so-called stainless steel around the stove's burners, the mimosas faded with each swipe. For an instant she missed the museum: the lab's hands-on work, her colleagues' gallows humor. Elena would take one look at *Schuylerhaugh* and shake her head. Paul would tell her to toss a coin. The artist in the clown suit would say, *It's how I keep from dying.*

She scrubbed harder. Even the kettle was spattered, and if her counter had space for a coffeemaker, she'd be scrubbing all night.... But Demi had a Krups. Whose idea was that—Adam's or Eve's? To an artist, every detail counted. Foliage creeping up on a manor house had meant something to Thomas Cole, because in a miniature universe like a painting everything had to count. Crime scene dioramas were miniature universes, too....

Ping. Probably Angela.

Lily rinsed out her sponge and began scrubbing the sink. Eve had scripted Demi's death in her micro-mini studio as an accident, but in Bliss Byrd's carefully curated and slightly larger universe, a real killer had played God.

Ping.

Downsizing was trendy. Micro-mini studios met Gen Z's wallet and needs; Bliss Byrd and her Baby Boomer clients thrilled to less is more. But what if the killer upsized? What if he went from a diorama to—

Ping. Lily grabbed her cell.

"Did Eve pony up?" Paul asked.

"The mimosas had gin."

He chuckled. "When's our date with that realtor?"

"Uh—"

"You made the appointment, right?" Paul asked.

"Of course!" The last bubble of mimosa evaporated. She hadn't even called Trudi yet. "We're meeting Tuesday, after the final diorama."

"Another dollhouse, eh?" He sounded less than enthusiastic.

"What if they're connected to the murders, Paul?"

"How?" he asked doubtfully.

"The dioramas are miniature crime scenes, right? Maybe Demi's micro-mini studio was a model for Bliss Byrd's tiny house."

"A *model?*"

"And Glenn's conservatory is Bruce Kemp's glass—"

"You're saying the houses were targets?" Paul laughed. "I've heard zany theories, darling, but—"

"Not just where they lived!" He was one step away from blowing her a kiss and hanging up for the night. Lily took a deep breath. "Humor me a second, Paul. Bruce was an engineer, Glenn a urologist—"

"Um, scientific backgrounds, bonsai and abstract art?"

"Collectors showcasing themselves!" Paul laughed again, but she plunged on. "Bliss was a declutterer, Demi crammed her entire existence into 300 square feet—"

"Glenn and Demi are *dolls*, Lily." He sighed. "God, I miss you. When this depo's over, I'm hopping a plane. I hope that realtor's good."

They hung up and she dialed Trudi.

Trudi Rood, the voicemail said. *Call you back!*

Too wired to sleep, Lily got out Jack's clippers and brush. He fled under the couch. She went to the bathroom for her robe. Soap rimed the drain and shower door. Windex, vinegar, baking soda... not as satisfying as grooming Jack or throwing a mimosa at *Schuylerhaugh*, but the mixture foamed as she poured it down the drain. With it, she saw her career go down too. But an assistant was in the budget, and there was a slush fund. Angela didn't have to know.... Impulsively, she grabbed her phone and texted Sasha Lazar at Yale.

Reinvigorated, Lily started on the shower door. The Windex streaked. Pity whoever had cleaned the gore from Bruce's textured wall and floor-to-ceiling glass! Hopefully not his housekeeper... That reminded her of the blood spatter in Glenn's domed jewelry box. As with the controlled humidity in a real conservatory, the spatter had been diluted by moisture inside the glass. Those dioramas were so damn realistic....

Ping! Sasha Lazar's bright eyes and silver bob lit Lily's cell. Yale art historians didn't sleep, they FaceTimed. "Lily!" she said with delight. "Another murder?"

"A Thomas Cole."

"Oh."

Lily filled her in on *Schuylerhaugh*.

"And what does the boss think?" Sasha had been Angela's professor and was her oldest friend.

"She can't know."

"Hmmn. Hudson River School..." Sasha clicked her teeth. "I may know someone." Lily pressed her hands together in silent prayer, and the professor ducked her chin modestly. "But I suspect a larger crisis of confidence."

Sasha was right. Whoever killed Bliss Byrd and Bruce Kemp wasn't God, not even over a miniature universe. He was mortal, and the dioramas were a little too close to the crime scenes to be coincidental. Johnson and Paul would never believe they were connected; hell, they didn't even think Bliss was murdered. But if the dioramas were clues to targets and locations, tomorrow would be the last one.

"Trust your eye," Sasha said crisply.

And get into the killer's head.

—

Lily was almost asleep when the phone rang.

"Tuesday afternoon," Trudi Rood said. "Where do we start?"

The final diorama would be—

"High rises," Lily said.

Chapter Fifteen

The tiny man in the black Speedo floated face-up. If he'd still had a face. Entombed in shimmering turquoise, he appeared to drift. Purple tendrils wafted from his head like a mermaid's hair, dissipating as they spread. Bright red blood saturated the grout in the tiles on the pool deck. A folded terrycloth robe sat on a lounge chair.

Johnson shrugged innocently. "Slipped?"

"Those tiles do look dangerous," Eve said encouragingly.

Guffaws from the cops in DPD's conference room.

Burned by his failure to identify the proper cause of Demi's death, Johnson was probably hedging his bets. But this was the final diorama, and Lily wondered about the odds of two out of three suspicious deaths being accidents. Johnson had nodded at Paul when they arrived but avoided her. Now she circled the diorama warily.

"Or he pissed somebody off," a detective said.

"Run with that." Eve was watching Lily out of the corner of her eye. "What do we know about Lance?" The dead doll in the Speedo.

"BMW sales manager," Bowles read from his script.

Eve hadn't given her one.

"Enemies?" Eve asked Bowles.

"Nada."

Adam's diorama ingeniously depicted a ten-story condo's top floor and rooftop pool. The lower floors were compressed like layers in a collapsed wedding cake, with tiny balconies dotting the perimeter like blobs of icing oozing out. The pool deck overhung the tenth floor; the rest of the roof had been cut away to reveal two units. Lily peered into them.

"Which unit is Lance's?" Eve asked.

One was neat but sparsely furnished, like a show model. The other had an unmade bed, a sink filled with wee-sized dishes, and cushions and clothes piled on the rug. Its balcony had a dilapidated bike and grease-spattered grill. A tiny flight of steps led from the hall between the units up to the pool. Lily pointed to the first unit. "Lance's."

Eve frowned. "Why?"

"The Speedo and robe. He was neat and trim."

Johnson nodded grudgingly. "He worked out at a gym on Broadway."

Adam had joined Paul at the back of the room. He waved to Lily.

"Friends?" Eve asked.

"A well-liked loner," Lily replied.

"Odd for a sales manager," Eve mused, "especially at a luxury brand like BMW."

"Ms. Sparks is right," Bowles said, ignoring Johnson's scathing look. "Co-workers liked Lance, but he kept to himself."

Lily didn't need a script; as with Demi in her micro-mini studio, she'd lived this one, too. High rises were impersonal and anonymous, way stations for divorcés and couples with no kids. Denser and less expensive than detached dwellings, they were crowded but lonely. Once a week in the elevator, you nodded at neighbors you never saw in the lobby.

Ping—Sasha again? Her last text had been a cryptic *Cavalry coming.* Lily glanced down hopefully. Trudi. *5 pm?* She texted back a thumb's-up and refocused on the diorama. "Who found Lance?" she asked.

"Couple in 6B," Bowles read. "Romantic midnight swim."

Snickers.

"How soon was he found?" Lily asked.

"Not long after he was whacked," Johnson replied.

Eve jumped in. "How can you tell?"

Johnson laughed grimly. "Couple days in a tub and you look like a pot of—"

Lily looked at the tendrils of blood eddying from Lance's head. Was the lack of decomposition at the time he was found a clue, or did Eve script her crimes around the limitations of her husband's craft? Decomp would be tough to render on a plastic figurine, but Adam had filled the pool with a kind of pourable faux water that didn't shrink or crack. Lance was glued, suspended like a fly in amber. If the dioramas were previews of real murders, would the killer's next victim be in a pool?

"Could be a red herring," Bowles said slyly.

Groans and hand slaps.

Eve waited for the merriment to die down. "Go back to Lance's unit."

"Young athletic guy," a detective commented. "He must've had a girl."

Johnson poked Bowles. "Not much of a bachelor pad, eh?"

Bowles blushed. "Everybody has a life."

"The face you show the world…" Eve hinted.

"Someone was with Lance at the pool!" Johnson said. "I mean, well obviously…"

Eve nodded enthusiastically.

"… but it was late at night. Maybe a guy, from the looks of it. Attacked him on the deck, shoved him in the water. Lance's face is gone. What do you shrinks call it—depersonalized?"

Anonymous, Lily thought, *like the condo itself.*

Now Johnson was on a roll. "Lance picks up a guy, they have a few beers, he makes a pass, guy picks up a bottle—"

Lily shook her head.

"What?" Johnson demanded.

"There's no bottles or glass." She glanced at Adam, who nodded almost imperceptibly. Architects were artists. Every detail meant something. "Lance owned his unit, right? Let's talk neighbors." She pointed to the second unit. "Unlicensed Airbnb."

"What the *fuck*—" Johnson said.

"Crash pad—look at the mess. Dirty dishes and clothes, that disgusting grill on the balcony. I bet Lance complained, maybe reported the owner to the condo board. High rises are risky enough without strangers parading in and out next door."

"But the pool—" Johnson protested.

Lily shrugged. "Lance liked to swim at night."

"*Alone?*"

"It's quieter."

"Maybe it was random!" Johnson said. "A robbery—"

Lily shook her head. "His unit's neat as a pin. As for the weapon…"

Eve wasn't smiling anymore. She was staring at Adam.

"…you'll find it under that pile of clothes on the Airbnb's rug," Lily said.

Adam grinned.

Chapter Sixteen

"Dazzling, eh?" Trudi Rood said proudly.

Dizzying was more like it. The Apex's penthouse had three walls of windows which looked down on the clouds. "Are there blinds?" Lily asked.

Trudi chuckled. She'd swung by Lily's condo in a black-and-white vintage coupe slightly bigger than a saddle shoe. Paul had taken one look and said he'd meet them downtown. Unoffended, Trudi texted him the address. She was older than her photo; her blonde hair was platinum on the way to silver, and she had matching jewelry and nails. Her only cosmetic work was her teeth. No chompers were that white and big.

A helicopter suddenly flew past.

"Shit," Paul said admiringly.

Lily ducked.

Trudi seemed hurt. "You said high rise in the heart of downtown. When the Broncos have a night game, you close the solar shades."

Forty floors down, office workers streamed to bars and restaurants like ants at a picnic. One group filed off to Union Station, where there was an upscale food court; another broke away and headed for Coors Field.

The Apex had its own bistro and athletic club and was right between Lily's lab and Paul's firm. If Trudi suspected the $13 million price tag for this condo was a tad rich for their blood, she didn't show it. How many times had she flipped this unit?

"Great location," Paul said nonchalantly. "Jack would love this."

"Your… stepson?" Trudi diplomatically directed her question midway between them.

Paul snickered. Lily pictured him and her cat at the window, staring at traffic for hours on end. Jack already did that, but thankfully this penthouse had no balcony.

"And privacy," Paul continued. He could prance naked to his heart's content. The only thing this high up was a neighboring skyscraper with something mounted on the roof. It looked like a telescope.

"Is that Hunter Merritt's condo building?" Lily asked.

Trudi nodded smugly. "Same developer, but we're two stories higher."

Paul was gazing at the sky—was that a satellite? "What if the elevator breaks down?" Lily asked.

"You take off your Manolo Blahniks and hike." Trudi wore sporty flats.

"And garbage?"

Trudi frowned. "Gar*bage*?"

Having once represented a condo developer who'd failed to insulate a trash chute, Lily had to ask. Whenever 31B's owner had thrown out a wine bottle, his neighbors heard it clatter thirty flights down. In that same luxury tower, the rooftop pool had sprung a leak. What had she been thinking? This jaunt with Trudi was ridiculous. "Paul—" she appealed. But he was transfixed by the view. The stars were fireflies he could reach out and grab. Him and Jack, masters of the universe.

Trudi was scrolling her cell.

Lily's cursory research had revealed that she'd been at four other firms. Trudi owned three places in Aspen and had sued and been sued for everything from barking dogs to running an unlicensed Airbnb. Paul was right; Denver was a small town. So what if Trudi dated Bill Byrd and was the exclusive leasing agent for a rapacious RiNo developer like the one who'd charged Demi God-knows-what for her lousy 300 square feet? That was no excuse for wasting a busy woman's time. And Paul's—if Lily could get him to leave.

Lily turned back to Trudi. "You come highly recommended," she said.

"Hunter?" The realtor kept scrolling. "Lawyers I get."

"And Adam and Eve Castle."

Trudi looked up sharply.

"You sold them their house," Lily continued. The one she'd flipped for two hundred grand?

Trudi shrugged. "Her, I like."

"And him?"

She laughed ruefully. "Starchitects are a pain in the ass, you wouldn't believe the punch lists." Paul had moved to another window. "Your first place, right? Let me guess: you like the twenty-four-hour front desk, he wants a three-car garage."

"Well—"

"He worries resale value, you're phobic about heights." Trudi sighed. "So cute together."

"Sorry to waste your time…"

"Not at all!" She chuckled, then dropped her voice to a stage whisper. "He doesn't want this either." Paul had moved to the restaurant-sized kitchen with the eight-burner range and stainless-steel suspended hood. The vats of spaghetti and chili he could cook! He circled the stove like he was facing off against it in a boxing ring.

"How can you tell?" Lily asked.

"That Viking range."

"But Paul loves—"

Trudi shook her head. "It's a Maserati. Guys have to crank that baby up till the roast's incinerated or the kitchen's in flames. Better to dream."

Lily couldn't help thinking about the crime scenes and dioramas. Real or dolls, each victim had lived some sort of fantasy. Demi in her micro-mini studio, Prosser a rung on her ladder up. Bliss Byrd in her tiny Highlands house, where there was no room for a man because each object had to earn its space. Lance in his glistening rooftop pool, shutting out the Airbnb next door as he floated and gazed at a diorama's stars. Bruce Kemp in his Cranmer Park glass showcase, inviting the world to look but not touch.

"But Hunter didn't dream," Lily said. "He bought."

Trudi peered at her curiously. "I assure you it wasn't the stove."

"Space for paintings?"

"Those awful abstracts of his? To think I introduced him to that fracker who collected them!" Trudi's laugh made her sapphires tear. "Shit, my contacts..." She got out a tissue to wipe them. "But Hunter's building does have one advantage."

"Yeah?" Lily asked.

"Rooftop clubroom with 360-degree views, accessible only to owners on the top two floors. Pool table, wet bar..." Exclusivity, privacy, control—master of the universe until some maniac clubbed him to death like poor little Lance! "Level with me, Lily. What're you really looking for? Curb appeal, sunny windows? Renovated or—"

Paul had finally finished exploring the three-chambered sink.

"Who pays $13 million for a clubroom?" Lily asked Trudi.

The realtor busied herself with her phone. "Ask Hunter Merritt."

Chapter Seventeen

This early on a weekday morning, LoDo was delivery trucks and lawyers balancing briefcases and Starbucks Trentas. Lily dodged a fellow carrying a large box of pastries to the corner café and parked. She grabbed her lunch from the passenger seat. Before Sasha's expert showed up, she needed to get a better handle on *Schuylerhaugh*. She fed the meter and turned.

A scruffy-looking man sat on the sidewalk outside the lab's door. His hair stuck out, his sneakers were stained, and his corduroy jacket was bald at the elbows. He carefully hoisted his beat-up backpack and rose to his feet. He was thin, with sharp features and dark stubble on his strong chin. Impulsively, Lily held out her brown bag. The man blinked at it curiously.

"Take it," she said. Cheese had been the only thing in her fridge besides eggs. "Please."

He scrutinized the bag like an artifact.

She shook it enticingly. "I made it myself. Swiss with mustard on rye."

Amusement flitted across his blade-like face. She was starting to feel foolish. Despite the stubble and wild hair, he didn't really look like he'd missed too many meals or was waiting for the weed shop next door to open. "I've had breakfast, thanks," he replied. He shifted his backpack. "Lily Sparks?"

"And you're…?"

"Raf Feldman. Sasha says you're in deep shit."

A prank? Maybe Gina, or God forbid Angela—But how would he know Sasha?

"I've come a long way," he continued mildly. "Can I at least look at your Cole?"

He didn't look like an art expert, certainly not a Hudson River School scholar. Nor did he seem surprised that Sasha had given her no warning. Lily unlocked the door and let them in. "Mr. Feldman," she began, "or is it—"

"Raf. Sasha says the Rensselaer's jackboot's at your throat."

"Well—"

"Is this it?" Setting his backpack on the floor, he strode to *Schuylerhaugh*. He stopped four paces from it and stared intently. With a haircut and a shave, he wouldn't be half-bad. Pretty damned attractive in fact.

"Can I get you an espresso?" Lily offered.

Grunting approval at the skylight, he took a step back. "Cole did damn few manor paintings. You see why." He shook his head ruefully. "He painted *Featherstonhaugh* for \$25. Four views."

Lily didn't know that painting, but the skylight was as pitiless to *Schuylerhaugh* as her bathroom mirror was to her when her roots needed a touchup. Suddenly she felt defensive of Cole's bastard child. "Mr. Feldman—" —professor, what?

"Raf."

"—I don't care how broke Cole was."

"You should."

"Why?"

He stepped forward and leaned in, nose inches from the canvas. In all of his back and forth, he hadn't disturbed so much as a speck of

Schuylerhaugh's dust. Maybe he really was an expert. Lily wheeled over the Harolux studio luminaire, the dimmable LED light on the height-adjustable stand, but he dismissed it with a wave. "The eighteenth century was a revolution in art. Colourmen experimented with primers that dried faster and canvases that could be stored and rolled."

So he knew his eighteenth-century colourmen; big deal; she did too. Had he been taking her politeness as defeat? With Angela and the Rensselaer breathing down her neck, the last thing she needed was a lecture. "Mr. Feldman—"

"But Cole was old school. He ground his own colors and used 'Catskill umber,' the dirt he found walking the trails. He had a chemist mix his varnish."

"Fascinating." She wasn't about to offer him her stereo magnifying binoculars. She could barely wait to pay his return ticket from her own pocket. "Let's cut to the chase, Raf."

He spun. "How the hell do you expect to conserve a Cole without knowing a damn thing about his technique?"

Asshole.

"Or the architecture of paintings," he continued. "They're built from the ground up—"

"I'm an art conservator, Mr. Feldman."

"—totally uncharacteristic of Cole—"

"Look," she interrupted. "I know the ground's disintegrating. Can we hand-courier it lined with stretcher bars from the Tate?"

He smiled maniacally. "What keeps you honest, Ms. Sparks?"

Fuck you!

"I'll make it easier," he said. "What makes you tick?"

"At this moment?"

"Yes."

"Getting this fucking painting out that door." *And you with it!*

The lab pulsed.

Raf turned from her, and his gaze roamed the lab like a ravenous beast. He shook his head derisively at the Resko combo electric easel and worktable with inclinable laminate surface and extendable edges, the studio trolleys nested like Russian dolls, the Deffner & Johann carbonized steel palette knives arrayed like chef's knives. He stopped at the stereo microscope with the swivel arm and camera. "Leica, I assume. You actually use it?"

Prick. "Every chance I get."

Turning finally to the coffee machine, he spoke with a weary contempt. "Was that in *Fine Arts Connoisseur*?"

Lily stared him down. *Damned if you'll get an espresso.*

He smiled weakly. "At least it's Italian."

She snickered.

He snorted.

They laughed so hard *Schuylerhaugh* quivered.

Lily made them coffee and brought it to her desk.

"I meant it before," Raf said. "What keeps you honest?"

"Besides Swiss on rye?" She cut the sandwich with a palette knife and gave him half. "My eye."

"Sasha mentioned something about that." He took a cautious bite, then began wolfing down the food. "What's so special about yours?"

"It's what I see," she explained, "the details, and how they add up. What's missing from the picture." Raf glanced up. "When I was a kid, we'd take these walks."

"Who?" He sounded intrigued.

"Dad and me. He'd ask what I saw, then we'd double back and he'd ask me what changed. It was a game," she added self-consciously, "but it trained my eye."

"Sounds cool."

Was he serious? "It was our thing after Mom died."

"Oh. Sorry." Raf accepted her half of the sandwich. "And that's how you became an art conservator?"

"Well, first I was a lawyer."

"No shit!" Was he making fun of her? "Lawyer, art conservator..." He leaned across the desk expectantly.

What did she know about Raf Feldman? Untamed hair, scruffy beard, cautious eyes that missed nothing. His quiet confidence as he advanced across the floor to *Schuylerhaugh*, the respect that made him stop just the right distance from the canvas. Sasha had steered him to her for a reason, and it wasn't just the Cole.

"What really interests me is solving murders," she said.

Raf nearly choked. "Come again?"

Lily told him about George Kurtz's killer, and the one who'd murdered actresses and thrown Angela under the SUV. He listened intently, asking few questions, and squinting to visualize details--the gorier, the better. "More fun than poor old *Schuylerhaugh*," he finally said. What would he make of the dioramas?

"And what about you?" she asked.

He shrugged. "I'm a romantic."

Lily nodded. "If not, what's the point?"

They laughed and toasted each other with their espresso. But the moment ended when Lily looked past him to the Cole. "I can't bullshit Angela. She's my best friend, and we've been through too much."

"That condition report will be nasty," he agreed. "Want me to sign it?"

"That bad?"

Raf shook his head. "It ain't even a Cole."

The one thing worse than it turning to dust.

"Prove it," Lily said.

His eyes hungrily swept the lab. "Do you have a simple lightbox?"

—

Lily gave Raf the spare key to the lab and went shopping. As she picked up deli meat for the lab's minifridge, her phone pinged.

4 pm 2moro, Trudi's text said. *@lab*, Lily texted back.

She FaceTimed Sasha and tried to sound pissed. "You could've warned me."

"About what?" Sasha asked. On screen, she waved to undergrads shouldering backpacks and pushing back chairs. Like them and Angela, had Raf Feldman once been her protégé too?

"I thought you were sending me an art historian."

"Oh, dear!" Sasha's eyes twinkled. "Raf's far too talented and restless for academia. He needs the money and can't resist an unknown Cole." She accepted a tardy assignment from a student with an icy nod, then turned back to Lily. "One thing he doesn't know—yet."

"That's hard to believe."

"Like you, Raf has a taste for crime. Maybe even murder." Sasha gave it a beat. "Oh, and Lily? Break it to him gently, dear."

Chapter Eighteen

Paul wrapped his towel around his waist and emerged from the shower stall. Adam Castle came out of the next one. With his sloping shoulders and soft belly, Adam didn't look like a swimmer.

"Thanks for the guest pass," Adam said. "It's been forever since I hit the pool."

"Been there." After the open-heart surgery, Paul feared he'd never swim again. It took getting back in the water to truly believe he'd survived—and Lily. His doc finally had to quit telling him to pace it on both scores.

"Great club," Adam continued. "Eve loves saunas."

The men's locker room was packed. Guys ran around bare-assed, ESPN blared from the wall, and some jerk had tried to preempt the last vacant sink by parking his dop kit there and then sneaking off to the shower. Paul moved the dop kit. The basin had whiskers and soap scum, its last user one of those kids who still expected Mom to clean up after him. He spritzed the sink with sanitizer and wiped the mirror.

Adam's eyes met his. "Quite a shindig at your firm the other night."

"Glad you could come," Paul said.

"I needed a good real estate guy.... Damn! How'd you get that?" He was looking at the scar.

"Sword fight." Paul was used to locker room stares, but nobody ever asked.

"Come on."

"Bum aorta. They got in fast." Paul blinked away the madman coming at him with the machete; the part he wanted to remember was Lily coming back to that shack for him. "Hate to disappoint you, Adam, but the FBI's a desk job." He ran his razor up his throat and went on autopilot. A three-hundred pounder lumbered up the Jacuzzi's steps to settle with a paperback under a *NO DIVING* sign. Since an elephant could drown in a puddle two inches deep, there was also a sign that read *WARNING: No Lifeguard on Duty*. What did the club's lawyers charge for that advice?

"Desk job?" Adam echoed doubtfully.

"Shoot-outs are few and far between," Paul replied.

"And private practice?"

Paul nicked himself. "If you like spending days in a conference room watching your client being grilled on shit you prepped him on for months." And staying awake by objecting to just enough of it to send your adversary down a rabbit hole.

Adam nodded knowingly. "Denver must be pretty tame after D.C."

Their eyes locked. "Lily's here," Paul said.

Adam chuckled. "What's it like living with a gal with such a discerning eye?"

A giant with a full black beard and a cue-bald head took the adjoining basin and began trimming his beard with nail scissors. Then he sprayed his head with Barbasol and shaved it. The beard and bald head reminded Paul of a pair of mutts he'd seen that morning at Starbucks: a big Hungarian with a coat like a stringy mop, tethered to a chihuahua with one eye blue and the other brown. In perfect synchrony, they'd barked and lunged at a passing poodle who ignored them. Was his career as washed up as those dogs on the leash and the giant with the Barbasol?

"Paul?" Adam prodded.

"Living together will be a helluva lot easier when we have a bigger bath."

Adam rinsed his razor. "Shouldn't be too hard to find."

They moved to the lockers. Some asshole had taken up the entire bench: sneakers, flipflops, dop kit, cell phone, towel, comb, toothbrush and paste, personal basketball—like a clown car, the guy kept pulling more stuff from his gym bag. Paul retrieved his pants and shirt from the clothes rack. He cared less about somebody stealing them than their losing their press. Was it too soon to surprise Lily with sushi again?

"Who's your realtor?" Adam asked.

"Trudi Rood."

Adam stiffened.

Paul turned. "Know her?"

Adam shrugged. "Eve dealt with her."

"Problem?"

"Nothing ethical. She's better for a certain type of client."

"Hunter Merritt likes her."

"That penthouse," Adam smirked. "I rest my case."

Did he pick up on some vibe with Lily at the firm the other night? *She came back for me,* Paul reminded himself. "We're not the high-rise type."

Adam nodded. "I can show you a couple of houses."

Why did Lily tell Trudi to start with high rises? Paul wondered. She was as scared of heights as she was of water, and this whole Trudi Rood business was starting to feel funny. "If Lily's happy, I'm happy."

Adam chuckled again. "Before CT, Eve and I had our own problems." Paul didn't bite.

"How'd you two meet?" Adam asked.

"She whipped my ass on a case." And showed him how hot it was to watch her bring down a killer with things nobody else saw.

Adam slipped his loafers on. "Time for a beer?"

"Raincheck," Paul replied. "Takeout duty tonight."

"Well, we're looking forward to tomorrow."

Paul turned again. "Tomorrow?"

"Dinner at Castle Keep. Eve said seven p.m. sharp. Something special planned."

What else didn't Lily tell him? But Adam seemed nice enough, and he and Eve were new to town. Denver wasn't as pretentious as D.C., but it was still hard breaking in.

"Lily won the bet," Adam continued. He saw Paul's confusion. "Lance's diorama—that BMW guy bludgeoned in the pool."

"Oh, yeah." Johnson had given him a ration of shit about those dollhouses. Now a particularly promising young recruit was agitating for more programs.

Adam followed Paul out. "She did miss one thing, though."

"Yeah?" Sushi tonight. Unagi—or bluefin?

"The club was under the sink, not in the pile of clothes."

"Club?" Paul asked.

"What the killer used." Adam waved goodbye to the on-duty manager. "Lily got the location wrong, but Eve didn't even know a weapon was there."

Chapter Nineteen

"Did you sleep here?" Lily asked Raf.

"What?" His stubble was gone, but he'd apparently shaved blind. He'd found a stand for the lightbox, and now he angled it parallel to *Schuylerhaugh*. She started to dread what was coming.

"Coffee?" she offered.

"Later."

She stowed the deli meat in the mini-fridge and locked the front door.

"Ready?" Raf inserted a thumb drive in the lightbox and rubbed his hands in anticipation.

The screen lit with a rugged nineteenth century landscape. In the foreground a lone tree trunk twisted. Behind it, clouds massed. "What do you see?" he asked.

"Nature's triumph over man."

Raf rolled his eyes. "*View of Featherstonhaugh Estate near Duanesburg,* 1826."

"I thought we were looking at manor portraits," she said.

"We are."

The next painting had more objects. "What do you see?" Raf repeated.

"Tree stumps and sheep, a lake, more clouds, a distant hill."

He shifted impatiently. "What doesn't stand out?"

The white speck on the hill. "A house?" Lily asked.

"Very good!" he cried. "*Landscape, the Seat of Mr. Featherstonhaugh in the Distance.*"

Lily stole a glance at *Schuylerhaugh*. Benjy Schuyler's ancestral home was decrepit, but it dominated the canvas. "Must we—"

Raf pulled up a third painting. "*The Woodchopper, Lake Featherstonhaugh.*"

This view of Featherston's estate did have a woodchopper—and sheep, even cows. The house itself was barely visible across the lake and through the trees. Lily heard Dad ask, *What's missing from this manor house picture?* She stifled a giggle. *The fucking house!*

Raf queued up another Cole. "*The Van Rensselaer Manor House,* 1841." An empty chair on a broad lawn, the house half-hidden behind a stand of trees. He turned to Lily expectantly.

She heard Dad again: *What do you see, Lily? Details, please...*

"Lily?" Raf said.

This was no longer a lark.

In sickening detail, her entire professional life unspooled. Law school, where *Details, please* got A's and offers from fancy firms. Her coup in recognizing Elena's looted watercolor was forged. *Nobody but you saw!* At the brink of partnership, thumbing her nose at her firm by resigning to become an art conservator. Then ten grueling years of art and chemistry and studio work and fellowships before the museum hired her. Conserving paintings and solving murders on the museum's dime and a hunch and a prayer, then quitting before her so-called perfect eye got her fired. Angela tossing her a lifeline by hiring her to run this lab. How could she have missed that *Schuylerhaugh* was fake?

Lily went to her desk and dropped her head in her hands.

"Don't you see?" Raf demanded.

There went Angela's Frederic Church. The Bierstadt. The Met's

Renoir. Raf had been her last hope. "Please, just go."

"Go?" Raf seemed surprised. "Don't you *see*?"

"That Cole didn't paint houses?" she said sullenly.

Now he was getting pissed. "Why do you think I hopped on a plane after Sasha called? House paintings represent status and power, but Cole was about nature's fearsomeness. Gnarled trees, gathering clouds—"

"Maybe Featherston didn't pay him enough to paint the damn house!" A cloud skittered across the skylight and eclipsed the noonday sun. Lily raised her hands in defeat.

Raf smiled imperiously across the desk. "No wonder you feel like an imposter."

That does it. "And what are you, a failed academic?" He wasn't in the Yale directory. "No wonder you can't get tenure."

His eyes blazed. "This isn't a lab, it's a set straight out of *Architectural Digest*."

Lily stood. "Get the fuck out!"

He pushed back his chair. "Want me to write and sign that condition report? I'll make it so Angela never knows how scared you were to call her painting out."

"Scared?" She trembled with fury.

"Even bad art's sacred to an artist, Lily. What's sacred to you?"

Raf shouldered his pack and walked out.

———

Lily threw away the cold cuts and wheeled the lightbox to its corner.

Her phone pinged and the lab's land line rang and rang. Ignoring them, she swept up *Schuylerhaugh*'s dust. With Raf gone, her fury turned to herself. What made her think she could solve real murders if she'd missed that a moldering paean to the pathetic Schuyler ancestral home was a fake? Clouds massed over the skylight—a thunderstorm or Raf Feldman's parting Bronx cheer... Somebody was banging at the door.

Raf.

"I was an asshole," he mumbled, "and it's not my first time."

She let him in. "I should've caught it."

"Not unless you were a Hudson River School scholar," he said consolingly. "Cole documented all of his commissions."

"But if I'd looked—"

Raf shook his head emphatically. "It's not your eye, Lily, and imposters don't care about truth. As for Angela—"

"She has a lot riding on *Schuylerhaugh*, Raf. We'd better be right."

He set down his backpack. "Before you stick your head under the guillotine, I'll show you what you're dying for."

—

Lily salvaged the cold cuts, and Raf wheeled the lightbox back to the easel.

"We'll take it from the ground up," he said.

Rain pattered on the skylight as they deconstructed *Schuylerhaugh*. Infrared studies of authentic Coles on Raf's thumb drive showed the artist had made underdrawings and used grids to transfer design elements from his sketches to his canvases.

"Like blueprints," Lily said, "or an architect's model." Raf nodded and zoomed in on the sky of an authentic Cole. Striations created rays from the setting sun. "He combed through the blue while it was wet," she marveled, "with a graining tool—"

"—for a faux wood finish!"

They high-fived.

They examined brushwork, impasto, imprimatura. Raf relented and let her pull out the stereo microscope. *Schuylerhaugh*'s green pigment had blackened and the vertical streaks were from lead acetate a cut-rate canvas maker had used to make it dry faster. In addition to the very un-Cole-like prominence of Schuyler's manor house, the painting's condition was simply too poor to be an authentic Thomas Cole. By the time they'd finished, the rain was done and sun slanted through the skylight, the beveled overhead panes casting a decidedly Cole-like grid on the tile floor.

"You said manor house paintings represent status and power," Lily said.

Raf nodded. "Like with Featherston's house, sometimes the painting is all that survives."

Adam Castle had said the same thing about Angela's baby dollhouse: the miniature replicas immortalized the homeowner and builder. And if buildings and paintings were built from the ground up, with models and blueprints, maybe crimes were too. Were the Castles' dioramas more than a teaching tool?

"About Angela…" Raf began.

They looked up at a figure in the doorway.

Chapter Twenty

Paul instantly processed the scene.

Lily at the lightbox, giving a guilty start. A scruffy mutt furtively popping out a thumb drive. Her wheeling the lightbox away. Him trying to stare Paul down with a manic grin.

"Paul!" Lily sounded surprised. So much for their meeting with Trudi Rood.

"Four p.m.," Paul said politely. "Did you forget?"

"What? No, of course not!" Disheveled, giddy. That coming-out-of-the-shower look meant only for Paul. What was on that thumb drive? Blushing—*blushing!*—she turned to the mutt. He looked like he'd used an eggbeater on his hair.

"Lily!" came a voice from the doorway. Angela with Eve Castle. "We were on our way—" Seeing the mutt, Angela stopped.

Lily looked from her to Eve to Paul, then slid protectively in front of the mutt. He stepped out from behind her and smiled craftily at Angela.

"Who are you?" Angela asked.

He offered his hand. "Raf—" he began.

"Professor—" Lily said.

"—Feldman."

Angela frowned.

"Colleague—" Lily said.

"—of Professor Lazar," he finished.

Angela brightened, then furrowed her brow. "I don't recall Sasha mentioning you."

"She wouldn't," Raf replied.

Angela turned to Lily. "Join us for cocktails? I'm dining with Benjy Schuyler at The Cactus Club tonight." She winced charmingly. "Overdone Beef Wellington, limp green beans, and potatoes whipped by the Marquis de Sade. Give me good news to wash down the pinot and antacid."

Lily and the mutt exchanged a glance. Eve was gaping at them like she'd stumbled onto a car wreck or mistakenly wandered into the opening of an experimental play. Everyone avoided the spectacularly ugly canvas on the easel. It was powdered with a mossy silt that squirmed. The Cole. Talk about a scrape... *Poor Lily*, Paul thought.

He jumped in. "The good news is, we're looking to buy a house!"

Eve clapped her hands.

"About time," Angela said approvingly. "Where's Johnson on Bliss Byrd's murder? If he doesn't get off his ass, I'll talk to the mayor and have his badge."

Focus. "He's working the case," Paul replied, "but Bill Byrd has an alibi."

"Am I late?" a voice bellowed. "Parking's hell!" Trudi Rood stood at the door, juggling her cell and an enormous tote. Angela peered at her suspiciously, and the realtor gaily waved back. "Trudi Rood."

Eve stiffened.

"Is that your real name?" the mutt asked Trudi.

Angela snickered.

Trudi gasped, then wagged her finger. "As of my last husband, and I do mean last. Where'd you say you're from?"

"Pittsburgh," the mutt replied.

Eve shook herself alive. "Why, CT's pilot program was in Pittsburgh!"

"I'm from Steel City too!" Trudi cried.

Eve blanched.

Steel City?

Angela rapped her cane. "We're late for cocktails."

Paul was starting to feel like he'd wandered into a bad comedy or crashed the Mad Hatter's tea party. But Eve was staring at Trudi with a fascination bordering on fear. What had Adam said? *Eve dealt with her.*

Trudi turned to Lily. "More high rises today? Hunter can show us his clubroom…"

Lily's eyes widened.

Pittsburgh, Hunter, clubroom. *What the fuck am I missing?*

"…or something smaller, low to the ground," Trudi finished.

Bliss Byrd's tiny house?

Trudi looked up at the skylight. "And glass, lots of glass…"

That bonsai diorama?

Paul shook his head. That's how it always was with Lily; hang around her long enough and you started thinking like her. He took her by the elbow. "Let's get going."

"Low to the ground, glass." Trudi scrolled her cell. "We're in luck, one just came on the market." She kept scrolling. "Or something more intimate. A darling carriage house popped up near the Country Club."

Angela guffawed. "The only thing a carriage house is good for is a nooner!"

Eve blanched.

Trudi rattled her keys like cat treats.

The mutt winked and rolled up his sleeves. "I'll hold down the fort."

Paul followed the women out. As he wedged himself into the backseat of Trudi's black-and-white bowling shoe, his questions boiled down to one.

Who is that mutt?

Chapter Twenty-One

As she climbed Castle Keep's steps, Lily wanted to be anywhere but there. After her cyclone ride with Raf and touring carriage houses with Trudi, she was on the verge of a migraine. Paul too seemed in a snit.

"Let's just get through this," he muttered as he rang the bell.

"Uh-oh," Adam said with a smile as he opened the door. "Looks like you two can use a drink."

"That'd help," Paul said tightly.

"Be right with you!" Eve called from the kitchen. Through that doorway came the scents of garlic and a roast.

Lily followed the men into the living room. Castle Keep was a stately older home on the fringes of the Country Club, and period details had been meticulously maintained, from crown moldings to a fireplace with an antique cast-iron inset. At a drink trolley, Adam mixed gin and tonics. The gin was strong. "Lovely place," she said gamely.

"Eve found it," Adam replied. He moved to the couch, and she and Paul followed.

"Why not design your own house?" she asked. Trudi had mentioned something about architects and punch lists.

"The Great Pyramid?" Adam laughed. "Cheops was immortal, not married."

On cue, Eve entered and perched beside him on the couch. Her cheeks were flushed and her ruffled apron made her look girlish. She sipped something colorless from a tall glass and fanned her face. The sun hadn't set and the house was stuffy. "I don't know what gave me the idea to cook a roast in this heat!" She kept looking in the direction of the front door.

"Can I help?" Lily asked.

"No, dear. Any luck with Trudi?"

Paul snorted. "She thinks we're giants or Lilliputians."

"The Goldilocks gambit!" Adam said. "First high rises, then carriage houses. Poor Trudi. She has no idea what you really want."

"Architects usually don't either," Eve reminded him gently.

Adam stared into his drink. "You get so caught up in your vision, you forget buildings are for people. You learn the hard way it's about them and not you."

Those Miami condos, Lily thought.

Eve patted his knee. "Adam's returning to his house-designing roots, but true artists never do anything twice."

"Start repeating yourself and you're dead." Adam seized his wife's hand and kissed it. "My clients don't know it, but they're getting a damn good shrink free of charge."

Eve pecked his cheek and rose. "I'll let Cheops give you the grand tour."

—

The Castles' garage was a high-end toyshop. Families of miniature tools hung neatly from a pegboard, bins of tiny landscape materials and furnishings lined the shelves, and a worktable took up most of the floor. Adam switched on the overhead light.

Lily gasped.

On the table, a three-foot tall glass obelisk floated in a sleek titanium frame. Like a diamond, the model for Adam's soaring Miami luxury tower seemed to endlessly refract light.

"Is that a helipad?" Paul asked.

"Just toys," Adam said diffidently as he plucked a tiny chopper from the roof and cradled it in his hands. "The best buildings should never be built."

There was a second, smaller object on the table. It was draped in a cloth.

"What's that?" Paul asked.

Adam brightened. "CT's next gig is Phoenix. Eve books them." He looked up at his wife, who'd joined them with a fresh drink. The roast must be done because Eve had taken off her apron. Her black jersey dress was the same style as she'd worn at the DPD, but this one clung to her curves.

"Show them, Adam," she said.

Theatrically he whisked away the cloth.

Lily's breath caught.

The little cottage had timber cladding, a stone chimney with decorative clay flue pots, and a steeply pitched roof. It belonged in a hamlet with a church with a tall steeple, and a locomotive steaming through the countryside. But something—

"Medieval chic," Adam said nostalgically. The roof's asymmetry did evoke thatching. "Tudor Revival was Anglo aristocracy for the middle class."

The cottage was evidently a work-in-progress—the interior was empty—but the ivy on the walls and junipers crowding the walk somehow suggested its best years were behind it. Lily felt the Castles watching her.

"Who lives there?" Eve asked.

"A widower," Lily blurted out.

Adam reared back in horror, and everyone laughed.

"The foliage," Lily explained, but it wasn't just that. "Pfitzers have taken over and he's let the lawn go."

"Lawn?" Paul said. His normal good humor had been restored by the company and gin, but the diorama ended at the front walk.

Eve nodded wisely. "You want a garden…"

Mom grew peonies. "…and sunlight and air."

Paul put his arm around her and squeezed. "Growing up on a farm in Iowa cured me of that. You can see for miles, but there's nothing to see."

Eve laughed. "Let's eat."

—

The roast was succulent. Adam was generous with the wine, and Eve stopped watching the door. By dessert, they'd moved from architecture to art to the local real estate market.

"You don't need Trudi," Adam insisted. "If a house has good bones—"

The door rang. Eve's hand fluttered to her hair.

"Solicitor," he said dismissively.

"They'll keep ringing," Eve fretted. She gestured to a silver pot on the sideboard. "Lily, be a dear…" She excused herself to get the door.

As Lily poured coffee, she heard low voices in the foyer. Then they abruptly stopped.

Adam glanced up from his cup and his face froze. Recomposing his expression into a smile, he stiffly rose. "Frank!" he said. "How long have you been in town?"

The broad-shoulder man in the doorway with the cropped steel hair smiled back. "The past week, giving lectures at DU." His iris linen shirt and navy sport coat nipped at the waist made him look like a military officer in civilian clothes. He advanced and held out his hand to Lily. His blue eyes pierced hers, and the air around him seemed to crackle. "Frank Gould."

Eve had obviously been expecting him, but given Frank's wattage and Adam's reaction, she'd been smart not to set the table for five. Now she pulled up a chair and bustled to get her guest a plate. Frank waited politely for her to set his place before taking his seat. As if suddenly remembering he was the host, Adam poured himself and Frank wine.

"How's Oregon?" he asked.

"Greyer than Steel City, which is why I've moved to Arizona, Adam." Frank winked at Eve as she served his roast beef rare—she must have known he liked it that way. He cut a bite and chewed precisely before slicing the next. "I'll never have another grad student as talented as your wife, but I'm running the Forensic Psych program at the med school in Phoenix."

"Sounds fascinating," Lily said. "I understand you're behind Castle Training."

Frank squinted, then laughed. "You give me far too much credit, my dear." He had a tall man's way of hunching his shoulders and craning his neck to make himself less intimidating. He smiled genially in the direction of his host, who'd abandoned his coffee entirely. "With Adam's talents as an architect, and Eve's insights into victims and offenders, using crime scene dioramas to train cops was a natural fit."

"Why houses?" Lily asked. "Crimes can happen anywhere."

Frank set down his fork. "Homes mirror and affect their inhabitants' psyches."

Demi's micro-mini studio—Bliss Byrd's tiny house. Glenn's conservatory—Bruce Kemp's glass house. Lance's rooftop pool—"How?" she demanded.

"Lily," Paul chided, and Adam nodded at him gratefully. Maybe she *was* trying to impress Frank.

"No, it's a great question." Frank pushed back his plate. "There's a whole body of work, peer-reviewed, of course—"—he smiled at Paul before returning to Lily—"—about how houses' physical features and social codes affect power dynamics."

Paul was incredulous. "Are you suggesting crimes are tied to *homes*?"

Frank grinned. Was he amused, or taking Paul's measure? "Unfortunately, we can't design an experiment—"

"Damn right!"

Frank nodded condescendingly. "But there's no doubt dwellings say a lot about victims, and victimology identifies offenders. That's Profiling

101." Finally having pegged Paul, he toasted him with the last of Adam's wine.

—

The party broke up late, and Paul hustled her to the car.

"That's one self-satisfied prick," he said.

Lily pecked him reassuringly on the cheek. "He's Adam's problem, not ours."

Chapter Twenty-Two

At six a.m., Cheesman Park belonged to joggers and dog walkers. As she waited for a large group to clear the intersection, Lily drummed her steering wheel. Accidentally she hit the horn, and a grey-haired runner in a knee brace flipped her off.

Paul had risen before her and declined coffee. He could drink ten truckdrivers under the table without a hangover, but this morning he wasn't exactly chipper. When she brought up last night and Frank, he'd rolled his eyes and muttered something about depos and D.C. When she asked about making another appointment with Trudi, he looked like he was about to flip both her and the realtor off.

Now a brigade of militant moms with strollers stood shoulder to shoulder at the crosswalk. A toddler clutched a giraffe. Did girls still play with dolls? Lily's mind wandered to the dioramas. No matter what Johnson said, it was a mistake to think of Frances Glessner Lee's progeny and Castle Training's creations as dollhouses; they were miniature crime scenes, with the dolls in them murdered. Was it a coincidence that those murders echoed real crimes which had been occurring since CT came to town?

Now Frank Gould had shown up, and his thesis about the power dynamics of domiciles had hit uncomfortably close to home. Just look at Dad's bungalow. Closeted rooms shunned by the sun, yellowed linoleum, and scarred Formica counters. Silent dinners and angry words—no wonder Mom tried to peel out the night she died! Since Dad moved to that retirement complex last year, he'd been happier than Lily had ever seen him. But the victims in the dioramas and the real houses lived alone. What was that power dynamic? Still waiting for the crosswalk to clear, she Googled Frank on her phone.

PhD in Clinical Psych from UCLA. Couple dozen papers in top-tier journals. Teaching awards from Tulane, Oregon and Carnegie Mellon. Students rated him off the charts.

Beep!

Flipping off the driver behind her, Lily bolted through the intersection and pulled to the curb. What was missing from Frank's picture?

No wives apparently, or exes—nor reported scandals or complaints. But there was a gap between college and grad school, and a tantalizing three-year hole between UCLA and Tulane. With cars and cyclists speeding past, Lily pulled up his first paper.

No Place Like Home: Modeling an Obedient Universe.

Despite the catchy title, the abstract made the need to create symmetry and order to survive hostile environments sound like a total snooze. The biographical squib identified the author as a decorated U.S. Air Force Colonel working at DOD. She squinted at the photo of a much younger Frank with short tapered black hair; even then his eyes were magnetic. The paper itself required special access.

Military training and DOD explained the gaps in Frank's CV, but did he still work for them off the books? Lily imagined him training himself to hunch his shoulders. What else did he adapt to or hide? His explanation of CT's origin, and his relationship with Eve, seemed too pat. And speaking of Pittsburgh—

Beep! A scrappy VW almost sideswiped her.

No, the likeness between a micro-mini studio and a tiny house, and a conservatory and a glass showplace, seemed too obvious to overlook. But two crimes still didn't make a pattern.

Scrolling, Lily found a feature article *The Pittsburgh Post-Gazette* had run on CT's pilot program. It was a fun spread, with photos of dioramas and an interview with Eve about Frances Glessner Lee. *We teach investigators to observe*, Eve told the reporter, *solving crimes is up to them*. Two days after that article, a prominent Pittsburgh couple had been slain in their North Side home. Rash of crime, a burglary-gone-bad, yadayada. No pix or address. Then a week later, an outraged editorial about the still-unsolved double murder being a poster child for an inept police force and CT being too little, too late....

Lights flashed in Lily's side mirror. She looked up at a *No Parking* sign and a motorcycle cop. Waving sheepishly, she pulled from the curb.

—

When Lily arrived at the lab, Raf was perched on a stool under the skylight. Hair tousled, backpack and coffee mug at his feet, he bent over a sketchpad in his lap. His pencil sped across the page.

"Raf?" she said.

Blindly he reached for the mug. Instead of coffee, it was filled with pencils. By touch, he selected a new one. Lily drew closer and looked over his shoulder. On the page were a cone and a sphere. Raf's pencil swiftly shaded and lit the sphere, each stroke bringing it more alive. *Far too talented for academia,* Sasha had said. He tore out the page and crumpled it up.

"No!" Lily cried.

Raf looked up. "It's just a sketch."

"But—"

"My daily object lesson, Lily. Every morning I limber up." He lobbed the crumpled paper at the waste basket. "It's a drill, like musical scales. If I don't practice, I get out of shape."

"Sasha didn't tell me."

"She wouldn't." Raf glanced at his watch and reached for his backpack.

He can't be leaving. "What's your style?" Lily quickly asked.

"Classical realism." He glanced at his watch again, and she felt a clutch of dread.

"Where's your studio?"

"New York." He shrugged diffidently. "Consulting and restoration gigs pay the rent, and they sell hot pretzels on the street."

"But you're so talented!" she exclaimed.

"That and two bucks buys a pretzel." Raf snorted. "An MFA's the new MBA, Lily—so much for truth and beauty." He gathered up his pencils and pad. "Art schools don't teach accuracy and proportion anymore, much less the big simple value pattern."

Lily pictured his mom giving him butcher paper and crayons. A big-eyed kid with pencil and pad at the Met, copying a Rembrandt drawing. The scruffy teenager with oils and portable easel standing before a Courbet. Sasha had been cryptic, but what *did* she say?

"Big simple value pattern?" Lily repeated.

"What draws you to a painting, the first impact it has." He finished packing his tools.

Don't go! "So you became a Hudson River School expert?"

"According to my PhD." He zipped up his backpack. "And my gig here's up."

"Who was she?" Lily asked desperately.

Raf looked up with amusement. "She?"

Frantically she tried to buy time. "The one you were an asshole to." *Sasha said…*

He laughed. "Too many to count."

"But I haven't paid you!"

"For what?" He sounded insulted. "Telling you *Schuylerhaugh*'s a third-rate effort by one of Cole's students? I'm a consultant, not a thief."

…he has a taste for crime!

Lily exhaled. "I'll reimburse your ticket—on one condition."

"Yeah?" he said doubtfully.

"Talking about pretzels makes me hungry." She grabbed her bag. "Let's get breakfast."

Chapter Twenty-Three

Live jazz, the discreet sign and a hidden stairway gave the lounge in Union Station's mezzanine a Gatsby vibe. Bars that required a reservation weren't Paul's thing, and he'd been surprised when Adam called. But Paul's smile always worked on hostesses, and Adam was waiting in a booth.

"Nice place," Paul said.

Last night at the Castles' had been pleasant enough until Eve's friend arrived. If Frank Gould was the surprise she'd planned, she clearly hadn't let her husband in on it. Tonight Adam still wore the same khakis and polo shirt, and behind the wire-rims his eyes fluttered. Paul knew a drowning man when he saw one.

As Adam studied the cocktail menu, the lounge bustled. The décor was granite, marble and brass, with wall sconces and tufted velvet sofas around low tables like a 1920s salon before the market crashed. Adam seemed to go for period detail, and the ladies here were better-looking than the guys at the gym. Finally he looked up. "Last night was awkward."

Nothing like having your wife's lover show up, Paul thought.

"I didn't know Frank was in town," Adam continued.

"Look, Adam, you don't have to—"

The server interrupted. Paul glanced at the menu—fancy drinks with cute names. They ordered some kind of dirty martini.... *Must be tough picking up stakes and relocating for your wife, and what do you say to a guy who'd been cuckolded in front of his dinner guests?*

"It's not what you think," Adam said. "I introduced them." Paul started to regret being alone with him in a booth. "Eve's practice was going downhill, I was flying back and forth to Miami. Stress was killing our marriage..."

The martinis arrived on silver trays. In a nod to Union Station's gilded age or modern first-class air, they came with ramekins of bar mix. Already mentally on tomorrow's flight to D.C., Paul took a healthy sip.

"...found her that graduate program with Frank. The old Carnegie Mellon tie."

Carnegie Mellon? *Our first training was in Pittsburgh.*

Adam leaned across the booth. "But he's not why I called."

"Adam—"

"It's CT." He fiddled with his lemon twist.

Paul exhaled. Lawsuits he could handle or refer.

"Remember that gal whose house blew up?" Adam continued. Bliss Byrd. He wasn't looking for a lawyer or a friend, he wanted an ex-FBI agent. "This sounds insane, but I think CT has a stalker."

Paul almost choked on his martini.

Across the balcony, the great hall's chandelier loomed like a maniacal moon. For a crazy moment, Paul was back in that penthouse with Trudi Rood. Distracted by helicopters and fog, missing something right in front of him. Bill Byrd... Hunter. Trudi Rood... Bliss. Instead of light, the giant orb threw sand in his eyes. Maybe he'd misheard Adam.

"It started in Pittsburgh," Adam said. "The stalking."

He's out of his frigging head.

But Pittsburgh—hadn't Frank Gould mentioned it? Frank reminded Paul of guys he knew in D.C.: ex-military with an education, the most dangerous kind. The Defense Advanced Research Projects Agency did science-fair type TED talks but had its hooks in everything from synthetic blood to mind-controlling nanobots. And that was just the shit that got out. At cocktail parties, DARPA guys stood in a corner and watched. Frank was chatty for a spook.

"CT gets lots of press," Adam went on. The *Post* had run a photo spread on the DPD gig. Did that story run before or after Bliss Byrd was killed? "We've put away more than one bad guy." He grabbed Paul's arm. "What if Frank's right, that crimes are tied to houses? What if the dioramas inspire some crazy—" Was he trying to incriminate Frank Gould?

There must be better ways to win back your wife.

Paul set down his drink. "How can I help you, Adam?"

"Look into cities with CT grants and unsolved murders," Adam begged. He started to signal for another round.

Paul quickly rose. "Morning flight."

—

On his way out, Paul fired off two texts.

The first was to a D.C. number.

DARPA. Frank Gould?

The second was local.

R U up?

Chapter Twenty-Four

Paul watched Johnson stroll into the bar on Colfax, tie askew, wearing a wifebeater under his thin polyester shirt. What a misnomer that cop-style undershirt was, at least insofar as Johnson went. He had three exes, none of whom he spoke badly of or appeared to miss. His only souvenir of marriage was an encyclopedic knowledge of Denver's seediest joints on Colfax and an aggravating tendency to play mother hen.

"She kick you out?" Johnson asked Paul.

"Sorry to disappoint you."

Johnson heaved himself onto a vinyl stool and motioned the tattooed barmaid for shots and chasers. "You're no fun since you started shacking up with blondie," he told Paul.

"You mean Lily?"

"Could of warned me she'd be at those fucking dollhouses." Johnson shifted on the sticky seat. "If I'd known I was going ten rounds with Laila Ali I'd of worn a steel jockstrap."

Paul laughed. "She says nice things about you."

"Yeah?" Yearning was all over Johnson's jowly face.

"We'll have you to dinner at our new place," Paul promised. Johnson liked spaghetti.

"First the dame, now a house." The cop shook his balding head. "I'll book the wake."

The drinks were cheap and strong, no more than two ingredients. Cash only. Paul stopped counting the number of patrons with no teeth. This was one cop dive where the barkeeps easily handled the clientele.

"So what's up?" Johnson asked.

"Bliss Byrd."

Johnson rolled his eyes. "Fumes from the mini-Cooper in the driveway, or a bad gas connection by her contractor ex. Was it Bill Byrd's fault she designed the windows to stay shut?"

"And nailed her own door?" Paul asked.

"I told you, it blew to smithereens."

Paul tossed back his shot. "Bruce Kemp."

Johnson winced. "First Byrd, now Kemp. Why bust my chops?"

"Lily knew Bruce, and Angela Kurtz knew Bliss. That's one degree of separation and two too many murders—"

"—unexplained deaths!"

"Shotgun blast to the head needs an explanation?" Paul demanded.

"Shit." A couple of ex-cons vacated a booth, and Johnson signaled the barmaid to bring the next round there. "I'll give you Kemp. Robbery—"

"Anything stolen?" Paul asked.

"—investors pissed about losing some deal—"

"Pointblank in the face?"

"—or home invasion. Kemp's fucking house was a fishbowl, for Chrissake!" Johnson eyed Paul over the rim of his shot glass. "There's no connection between Bliss Byrd and Bruce. What's really going on?"

"CT."

Paul laid it all out for him, but he wasn't sure he himself believed it. The similarities between the dioramas and the crime scenes were intriguing, but the FBI in him needed more than coincidence. Lily's copycat theory wouldn't convince a golden retriever, much less a bleary Saint Bernard like Johnson. As for Adam saying CT had a stalker—

The detective leaned back. "Uh-huh. As I recall, you wrote DPD's grant proposal for CT because I, a functioning illiterate—"

"Did CT approach you?" Paul asked.

"Maybe."

DPD had applied for that grant six months ago. When did the Castles start planning to move to Denver? Conducting a program on their new home turf made sense, but if the dioramas inspired a killer, Paul needed to know the ramp-up time—when Adam and Eve decided which crime scenes to model, how long they took to build. And who outside CT knew. "Did they tell you what the dioramas would be in advance?"

"A surprise." Johnson chuckled. "Look, Paul, I know you want to impress her—"

"I'm not Adam Castle!"

"What?" Johnson pulled out a wad of cash. "Let's get you some food." A rancid scent wafted from the bar. "I'm not talking those franks in the crockpot. There's an all-night breakfast—"

"I'm not hungry!" The bar had caught a second wave of walk-ins off Colfax. Older, sadder than the clown art on the walls. Paul had an early morning flight. He tried again. "Look, I don't know if there's a connection or not. But what if it happened before?"

Johnson laughed indulgently. "Cold cases, like where?"

Carnegie Mellon. Pittsburgh—the mother ship. "Do you have a friend in Steel City?" Paul asked.

Johnson snorted. "I'm a Broncos fan. Besides, cold cases can molder for years."

Paul pulled up CT's website. "Their pilot in Pittsburgh was two years ago. Every city has a cold case database—"

"Better than that." Johnson's thumbs tap-danced over his own tiny keyboard. He stopped, frowned, typed some more. He waved his phone triumphantly. "Detective Lonnie Greene, PBP. We met at an FLETC program on CSI Advanced Forensic Techniques. That's Federal Law Enforcement—"

"I know what it is."

Johnson grinned at Paul's surprise. "Yeah, and I took typing at South High. I even know spellcheck. But it was sure fun watching you sweat over CT's grant—"

"Shit." Paul rose from the booth. "Call Greene."

"What's in it for him?" Johnson asked.

"Besides solving a shitload of cold cases?" Paul scrolled flights on his phone. "I'm seeing a client tomorrow afternoon, but I can stop in Pittsburgh on the way back. Tell Greene I'll buy him dinner."

Johnson doubled the barmaid's tip. "Find me a cheap flight and I'll come for the ride."

Chapter Twenty-Five

DPD's desk sergeant recognized Lily. "Johnson's not here."

"What a shame!" She'd counted on it, this early on a Saturday morning. "Think he'd mind us taking another peek at those dollhouses?" The cop gave Raf a once-over. He was wearing a clean shirt and one of Paul's older ties, and she'd told him to keep his mouth shut. "Art student interning with me this summer," she explained. "Next fall he's doing a special elective on arts and crafts in nineteenth century urban habitats—"

The sarge yawned and waved them through.

The three dioramas straddled the conference table like continents mashed together on a pre-tectonic shift map. Candy wrappers and a dented Diet Coke can compounded Lily's sensory overload. As she struggled to reorient herself, Raf strode to the diorama with the rooftop pool. He pointed to the blood streaming from the Lance doll's head.

"Seaweed!" he cried. "Gory absurdist art."

The soda can's red and silver drew Lily's eye to the Krups in Demi's micro-mini studio, and order slowly prevailed. "Start here," she instructed him. "What do you see?"

Reluctantly he sauntered over. "Early twenty-first century—"

"Don't be smart, Raf."

"I'm an intern," he groused, "remind me why it's Saturday and I'm in a tie."

Lily smiled painfully. "To test my thesis that the dioramas are blueprints for real murders so we can stop the next one from happening. This isn't a game."

"Damn." Raf turned to Demi's diorama. "Dead doll, book—is that some kind of law thing? —coffeemaker, cat, frumpy blue dress-for-success—"

"What's hiding in plain sight?" Lily tried.

Raf groaned. "Not that old saw!"

"Then think like an art historian or killer," she said, "whichever comes more naturally."

Raf grinned wolfishly. "The killer in me likes Demi's uncurtained bay window." He stepped back for a view of the three models together. "The artist admires the contradictions these dioramas achieve. The scale invites you in, but you can't fully enter. Peering behind windows and through doors makes you want to reach into the frame."

"No art-crit shit," Lily said peevishly. "Composition, narrative..."

"Hmmn." Raf scrutinized Demi's digs with the attention he'd given *Schuylerhaugh*. "Balanced and symmetric, objects spread evenly across the space." He moved the Diet Coke can next to that diorama. "Scale and proportion look right..." He frowned.

"What?" she demanded.

"The center of interest should be Demi, but she recedes into the space. Like the house in an authentic Cole, she's an afterthought." Raf rattled the can. "But we're going about this the wrong way, Lily. If you want narrative, let's view all three dioramas as a triptych. And then—"

"—compare them to the crime scenes!"

They circled the table slowly, like musical chairs.

Lily abruptly stopped at the bonsai conservatory. Glenn had fallen away from the pedestal for the prize-winning juniper grove, and the maze of benches seemed to dwarf him. The victims in these crime scene dioramas didn't own their space, their killers did. Of course, the models had been built by an architect, not a criminologist. But there was something about those benches. She stood back and looked straight down. Benches… rows… shapes, like what? Manicured shrubs, landscaped, manipulated… Suddenly she had it.

"What?" Raf said.

"The benches form a labyrinth."

"So?"

"The same pattern as the walls at Bruce's soirée!"

They turned to Lance's condo building.

"Two centers of energy," Raf mused, "the pool and the killer's Airbnb."

Lily saw what he meant. The victim's neatnik unit, and poor Lance himself, again were beside the point. But the turquoise water was vibrantly alive. The pool and the robe on the lounge chair seemed to issue an invitation.

"Miss Sparks?"

Bowles stood in the doorway. Clutching a brown bag, an apple and a Diet Coke, the beetle-browed rookie looked barely old enough to shave. Guiltily he swept the old soda can and candy wrappers off the table. "I sneak in here on breaks," he said. "Johnson's usually here early Saturday, but he signed out." He gestured sadly at the dioramas. "They're getting ready to auction them off."

"Do you have a favorite?" Raf asked.

"Lance's clubhouse." A blush crept up Bowles' downy cheeks. "Girls go clubbing to dance, guys to score," he explained. "A few drinks, and the anxiety skyrockets. If you want to get serious, you need someplace more private."

Lily gazed at the pool through the rookie's eyes. Clubbing—a Hugh Hefner fantasy for a twenty-buck cover charge. But Bowles was experienced enough to know he needed intimacy to score. Was the prospect of a rooftop clubroom inviting to a killer? Hunter Merritt had a penthouse. Maybe it was time to take him up on his invitation for a tour.

Bowles popped his Diet Coke and unwrapped a sandwich. He offered Lily his chips and gave Raf the apple. "What're you looking for?" he asked.

"Patterns between the dioramas and murders," Lily replied.

Over their snack, they debated whether realty signs and Krups and cats were coincidences or clues, if moveable walls and garden benches could form labyrinths, and whether bonsai cultivators and renewable-energy czars were technically green lovers. But the victims had no connections to each other.

"Trudi Rood knew Bliss and Bruce," Lily argued. "Maybe she's the killer."

Raf snorted. "If they were beaten to death with a cell phone or a tote."

Bowles looked baffled.

"Bill Byrd's realtor," Lily explained. "Trudi introduced Bruce to a lawyer who collects art."

The rookie scowled. "Women whack exes, not clients. Besides, if the dioramas are connected to real crimes, this killer's too smart to leave clues as obvious as coffeemakers and cats and fracking fluid."

Raf pitched his apple core in the trash. "I say we're looking too hard."

"The murders can't be random," Lily insisted. "If Trudi's not the killer—"

Raf shook his head emphatically. "What's missing is a big simple value pattern."

"Big simple…?" Bowles asked.

"What draws you to a painting," Lily said. "Here, the dioramas."

"What if there *is* no pattern?" Bowles asked.

"Postmodernism," Raf muttered.

Bowles went to the table. "Twenty-something legal assistant and middle-aged decluttering coach in tiny spaces. Retired urologist-bonsai-guru and green-energy-art-czar in glass houses. BMW sales manager who takes midnight swims in his rooftop clubhouse."

Raf nodded grudgingly. "Symmetry and narrative."

"The killer must know these houses," Lily argued.

"We've been through this," Raf said. "If it's a triptych…"

"…who's victim number three?" Bowles asked.

Lily joined them at the table, and they stalked the dioramas together. This time she stopped at Lance's rooftop roost: a successful BMW sales manager clubbed in a clubhouse. What was hiding in plain sight? Trudi knew the real victims and their houses. If she wasn't the killer… "High-powered saleswoman at the top of her game!"

"What?" Raf demanded.

"I've got to warn Trudi."

———

Lily texted Trudi. *WhereRU?*

Open house! Trudi shot back.

The showing was in Hilltop, a few blocks from Bruce Kemp's. Pulling up to the ocher stucco palazzo, Lily saw a Mercedes sedan drive off. Trudi stood on the front steps, fanning herself with a glossy brochure. "I thought you and Paul wanted something smaller," she said. "Fantastic buy, though—all the options. Original owners put in twice—"

"I'm not here for the house," Lily told her.

Trudi waved to a couple approaching in a luxury SUV. "Putzes," she muttered as they coasted by.

"You're in danger," Lily said.

"Of not making a sale?" Trudi laughed. "It's been a madhouse."

"Do you live alone?"

"Since I put Nair in my ex's Rogaine." A group of ladies with no business wearing Lycra strode purposefully up the sidewalk. Trudi fanned herself harder. "Premature welcome wagon, neighbors dying for a peek."

"Trudi, I'm serious. Where do you live?"

She turned. "What?"

"Someone may be trying to kill you."

"Jesus," Trudi muttered. "Not again."

Had she been warned?

Trudi took Lily's hand. "Come inside, the AC bill's horrendous." Voices echoed down the staircase and caromed off the empty rooms on the cavernous ground floor. How long had this mausoleum been on the market? A deserted— "Clients mistake us for priests or shrinks," Trudi assured her, "but whatever you tell me's confidential."

"It's not about me, Trudi," Lily began.

The welcome-wagoneers were sniffing around a marble fireplace.

"Good thing we hide the valuables," Trudi muttered.

"Goddammit, Trudi, listen!" Lily said.

Wide-eyed, the looky-loos scurried towards the kitchen.

"Costing me a sale always gets my attention." Trudi's face softened. "You have it for ninety seconds before a real buyer comes down those stairs." She led Lily to a dining room where they sat across a mahogany table.

"You knew Bliss Byrd, right?" Lily began.

"Is this about Bill?" Trudi started to rise. "Because—"

"And Bruce Kemp. They're both dead."

Trudi laughed. "We comb obits for our next clients, not the last." Voices were in the next room. "Gotta run, hon."

God knew what—or who—could be waiting in the basement. "Is someone closing up with you, Trudi, or picking you up?"

Trudi shook her head pityingly. "Honey, I've been pushing properties since I was a girl in Steel City."

"Can we talk tonight?" Lily begged.

"I'm heading for Aspen and a guy hotter than Bill Byrd."

"Who?" Lily demanded.

In the doorway a woman in Dior cat-style shades stood with a couple in tennis outfits.

Trudi smoothly rose. "Adele! And this time you brought clients…."

Chapter Twenty-Six

Paul rendezvoused with Johnson at Pit International's Cinnabon, and Greene picked them up outside the baggage claim. Greene was Johnson, right down to the Crown Victoria, stained tie, and polyester pants. Johnson wanted a cheesesteak, but with Paul's promise of an early dinner and a cigar, Greene drove them to the scene of his city's most notorious unsolved murder.

"Pittsburgh box." Greene gazed almost fondly at the stately Foursquare with the covered porch and hipped roof. "Sears used to sell 'em from a catalog."

"Didn't know you was an architect," Johnson groused.

"When a vic's on City Council and they're debating PBOP budget cuts, I'm the fucking Encyclopedia Britannica," Greene replied. "Plus it's on the historic register."

Paul stared at the well-kept older home. This leafy upscale neighborhood seemed an unlikely place for a brutal double homicide. Why wasn't it solved? "Show me the diorama again," he said.

Greene pulled it up on his cell. Pittsburgh had been CT's first training site, and the diorama's relative lack of sophistication showed. The second floor and a section of roof had been sawn away to reveal a middle-aged couple sprawled crudely on the living room floor, apparently shot in the head.

"Where's the gun?" Paul asked.

Greene even scowled like Johnson. "Eve Castle had fun with that." He zoomed in on a tiny revolver peeking out from under the diorama's couch. "Two shots, no GSR, gun skidded on the hardwood floor."

Johnson's stomach rumbled.

Paul looked up at the real house. The brick was sandblasted and the trim and gabled dormers were painted a proud cranberry and forest green. The neighboring houses were on spacious lots. Muggy and overcast as it was, he expected kids to be playing ball or pulling wheelies on the newly paved blacktop. But the stillness was as oppressive as the heat.

"Vacation homes and summer camp," Greene explained. "Folks around here can afford 'em."

The homicide had occurred this time of year, almost to the day. Did the killer case the neighborhood and find it deserted? "Was there an alarm system?" Paul asked.

Greene nodded. "The vics put everything they had into this place. Wife was a muckety-muck at Carnegie Mellon."

"Psych department?" Paul asked. Long shot, but maybe she knew Frank Gould.

"She ran the cognitive development program," Greene replied.

Johnson rolled his eyes.

"How kids figure stuff out," Paul explained to him.

"Aha!" Johnson said triumphantly. "If the vic was working with crazy kids, maybe she turned over the wrong rock."

Greene chuckled. "We eliminated the pre-K crowd from our suspect list." He turned serious. "This was no break-in gone bad. The ME says they were killed right after dinner. I dunno about Denver, but no Pittsburgh burglar worth his salt breaks in with people at home."

Paul nodded. "Enemies?"

"Besides disgruntled grad students and cops pissed about a hiring freeze?" Greene said.

"But it's a double homicide!" Johnson exclaimed. He still thought Paul's theories about copycats and stalkers were batshit. "I don't see—"

"The diorama made local news and the bodies were found two days later," Greene replied testily. "I'm six months from retirement. Till then I'm open to any lead, no matter how nuts."

Johnson made a peace sign. "Well, now that we've had our look—"

"Who lives here now?" Paul asked. The neighbors must be used to rubbernecks, but they'd been here twenty minutes and there was still no sign of life.

"It's been on and off the market," Greene said. "The couple's kids won't go near it."

Paul sighed. Pittsburgh was coming up empty, and if Lily found out about this jaunt with Johnson he'd never hear the end of it. But there was something eerie about this place. The lawn was tended and the boxwoods neatly clipped, but the trim was fading and a porch rail looked loose. The swing waited to be claimed, like the robe on the lounge chair at the rooftop pool in that DPD diorama.

Greene jiggled the house keys. "Shall we?"

—

No cleaning crew could erase the stink of death.

Inside the Foursquare, mildew and decay floated over biohazard-grade solvents. Blood had been scrubbed away, and newer planks replaced sections of oak that had been cut from the living room floor. The only remnant of the family who'd lived here was the faint odor of a pet. As the men's footsteps echoed through empty rooms, even Johnson was silent. The tour ended back in the front yard. Still no neighbors or kids.

"This place was targeted," Paul said.

Greene chuckled. "Maybe a burglar was looking for coins."

"Coins?" Johnson asked.

"This ain't our only unsolved crime," Greene said with an odd professional pride. "A husband was shot in the den of an older split-level across town. When we tore the bloody carpet out, we found old coins. Some contractor's idea of a joke." He chuckled again. "They say every house has a story."

"What were the other dioramas?" Paul asked.

"CT's?" Greene thought. "Well, I'll be damned!"

"You and me both if I don't get some chow—" Johnson began.

"There *was* a split level," Greene recalled. "Didn't connect it because the vic in that diorama was a dame."

"Do you still have it?" Paul asked. What would he find if he tweezed up the tiny carpet?

Greene shook his head. "Auctioned 'em all off in a PBA charity drive."

"Same bidder?"

Greene rolled his eyes at Johnson, then turned back to Paul. "Look, son, even I know when I'm grasping at straws."

And what would it prove anyway? Paul thought. CT's connection to Denver's murders was becoming increasingly tenuous, and he was concerned about Johnson. The old cop was sweating and his color seemed off. Paul climbed into the backseat to give him the AC. Greene had made an early reservation at the swankest cigar bar and restaurant in town.

"Adam Castle might know who bought 'em," Greene said consolingly. "Steel City boy, you know."

"What?" Paul leaned over the front seat.

"CT's launch was a homecoming," Greene said.

Paul met Johnson's eyes in the mirror.

"Adam's dad worked the railroad," Greene continued. "The steel mills collapsed and he was downsized right out of a job. CT's launch was local kid made good, it was in all the papers."

Johnson cleared his throat. "Paul's too shy to ask, but can we drive by Adam's old house?"

Chapter Twenty-Seven

As the elevator torpedoed up the shaft, Paul tapped his foot impatiently. Lily never used her own condo's clubroom, but she seemed obsessed with Hunter Merritt's. Obsessed enough to get Trudi Rood to finagle a tour and him to take the afternoon off by promising they'd make an offer on a house. On his way to meet her and Trudi here, he'd stopped by Hunter's office to give him a heads-up that they were coming, but his secretary claimed he was in Aspen. Thank God.

Paul was in no position to complain. He still smelled those old homicide cops' cigar smoke, and his ribs were sore from being poked. Urban renewal had downsized Adam Castle's boyhood home to a patch of crabgrass. And all the way home from Pittsburgh he'd sat next to Johnson. *When you gonna quit letting that little blonde lead you down blind alleys?* the old detective said.

Trudi, too, seemed bemused by Lily's demand. Something was off between them; their chattiness felt strained, and when Trudi keyed the elevator with Hunter's access code, she'd winked sympathetically at Paul. He'd given up guessing her age but respected her doggedness; after the clubroom they were touring parkway scrapes…. By habit, Paul scanned the elevator for security cameras but found none. The steel door whisked open.

"Ta-*da!*" Trudi trilled.

Hunter's penthouse delivered that Master-of-the-Universe jolt. Paul could look down on clouds in the buff and not worry about the widow next door timing how often and long he and Lily had sex. He could cook gallons of chili on a range powerful enough to launch a rocket ship, but this was getting old.

"Is this what you want?" Trudi asked.

He wanted to quit jetting to D.C. to defend banks that laundered Russian mob money through art and real estate in Miami and New York. He wanted three nights in a row with Lily, without the Castles or Angela or Trudi or Hunter or Johnson. A kitchen with a normal stove, a refrigerator big enough for real food and beer, and a bathroom with two sinks.

"Master suite's this way," Trudi said.

Was it true about Hunter and managing partner Ferguson's third wife? Paul had covered for his horny friend at that all-day partners meeting two weeks ago. He glanced at Lily, hoping she was ready to call this quits. But she was looking at a trio of gargantuan abstracts like the one in Hunter's office.

"Quite a collection," Lily said.

Trudi snorted. "One's enough for me. That purple swoosh gets old."

"They're an investment," Lily said, but her eyes were darting.

Paul sighed. "Where's the clubroom?"

Trudi's wink was twitchy, out-of-sync—tough to tell if she meant it for him, or them both. Paul rubbed his eyes. Too many flights and late nights. Was Johnson right, was he trying to impress Lily with that wild goose chase to Pittsburgh? He was ready to buy the next place Trudi showed them.

"Exclusive access for top two floors," she was saying. "Pool table, wet bar, Jacuzzi…"

For Fergie's wife and all the others waiting to be fucked. Paul almost pitied Hunter. The elevator whisked them up another two floors. The door opened and Trudi paused for oohs and aahs.

The clubroom was Hunter's penthouse with a balcony and billiards table. A powder room was discreetly partitioned off, and the only seating was bar stools and a deep plush couch with a fur throw. Paul glanced at the ceiling. The track lighting was probably wired for security cameras, but ten to one they were disconnected. At the wet bar a wine bottle stood open.

Trudi frowned. "I'll call maintenance."

Through a wall of glass, the sky was a cloudless blue. Sunlight shimmered off skyscrapers like a breeze on a pool. "Billiards," Paul murmured, "not pool." The felted table had no pockets.

"What?" Trudi was scrolling on her phone.

Out-sized balls on the felt. Even the billiard balls… The balcony door was ajar. At the threshold, Paul saw a black suede men's loafer. A familiar smell wafted over. Lily was heading for the balcony. He grabbed her arm.

"Go," he said.

"But—"

If she saw what water did to a body, she'd never get it out of her head. Paul pushed her and Trudi to the elevator. "Wait downstairs."

"For what?" Lily asked.

"Johnson."

She stared at him. He kissed her hard and stabbed the lobby button. The door slid shut.

From the smell, Hunter had been stewing awhile.

With his cell phone, Paul shot the loafer and balcony door. He doubted there'd be prints, but he used his hanky to slide the door open. The other loafer was on the step leading up to the Jacuzzi. Now the stench hit him like a punch. Who knew there were insects this high? Hanky at mouth and nose, he approached.

Quickly he turned away.

A robe monogrammed *HM* was draped on a chair by a table with two half-empty glasses of wine. Paul shot a close-up of a smudged rim. Lipstick? Pink. There'd been a nastier rumor about a legal assistant who'd abruptly left the firm.

The clock was ticking on how long he could delay calling Johnson. But he owed Hunter this much. He knelt and lifted the hem of his robe. Underneath it was a brass key—some kind of game? Three inches long, with a flat head and a square tip. He took a shot of it. The late afternoon sun hit the Jacuzzi. The stench was overpowering.

He rose and texted Johnson the address. *Bring 4en6.*

Johnson pinged back. *Whafuck?*

Paul pocketed his phone. On his way out he looked.

The red teemed.

Poor Johnson and his crew.

Chapter Twenty-Eight

"Another?" the bartender asked.

"Absolut-ly."

If the drinks here were the best in town, Lily wouldn't know it.

Built on the ruins of a demolished post office and accessed through an unmarked door with a gold bell in the alley behind one of the mammoth new hotels that had laid waste to Cherry Creek, there was nothing sexy about this cocktail bar. Feasting off demolished galleries and boutiques, it was a vampire's lair.

There was one human, however, in the form of a bartender, and he was generous with the hundred-proof. Lily closed her eyes to stop the neon-lit fixture over the bar from spinning. Before Paul had dragged her out of Hunter's clubroom, she'd glimpsed something unspeakable. It must have shown on her face because Trudi didn't ask what she saw.

Johnson had met them in the lobby. "Wait here," he'd said tersely, then left to grill the shaken concierge and security guard who looked like he'd been rudely woken from a nap. The paunchy detective stationed men at the lobby doors to check and record IDs before irate residents and guests entered or left. Bowles had sidled over.

"Hunter Merritt?" she asked him.

Bowles grimaced. "Two days in a hot tub—"

"—Lance's pool—"

"—in a rooftop clubroom."

Their eyes locked. Instead of playing games at DPD Saturday morning, what if they'd—

"Come," Johnson barked at Bowles. He turned to Lily. "Stay."

"I'm not a dog!" she protested.

"Sit!" Johnson turned on his heel and went to the elevator.

Trudi left.

Finally the elevator pinged and Paul emerged.

Lily ran to him.

He raised his hands, signaling not to approach. "I told Johnson he can interview you tomorrow." Sliding his billfold from his breast pocket with his forefinger and thumb, he held it out to her. "Call a Lyft."

"But—"

He stepped back. "I'll see you at home."

At the condo later, Paul had balled up his suit and shirt and left them in the hall outside the door. He went into the bathroom and closed the door. The shower ran full blast for twenty minutes. When he emerged, he pulled on Levi's and sneakers.

"Where are you—" she began.

He kissed her on the head. "Partner meeting. Don't wait up."

"But you need something to eat!"

He'd smiled queasily. "I'll pass."

Now, as Lily waited for Eve Castle to show, the vodka went down like water. She knew—and Bowles knew—that Hunter Merritt didn't need to die. The dioramas were blueprints for murders, and they'd had everything but the next victim's name. How could she have thought it would be Trudi?

Big simple value pattern? It had stared her right in the face. Demi's micro-mini studio mirrored Bliss Byrd's tiny house down to the Krups and the cat. Glenn cultivated bonsai like Bruce Kemp did artists; the showcases they lived in were literally glass houses, and the bonsai benches in Glenn's diorama echoed the real walls at Bruce's soirée. Hunter bought paintings from Bruce and represented Bill Byrd. How fucking hard was it to predict that BMW manager Lance's tryst in the pourable faux water of his tiny rooftop pool inspired that randy lawyer's murder in a Jacuzzi in his fuck-pad on the forty-first floor?

Now the question was *who*.

In the mirror, Lily watched Eve enter the bar. She nodded effusively to the doorwoman and picked her way across the dark floor. Eve had suggested this bar; Lily never heard of it. But in speakeasies not just drinks were spilled, and if CT's dioramas inspired a killer, she was willing to bet this had happened before.

"Lily!" Eve smiled wryly at the empty glass.

"Pittsburgh," Lily replied.

"I'll have what she's having," Eve told the bartender. While he served her, she watched Lily in the mirror over the bar. "Adam's inconsolable. Hunter and Paul were his only friends." Had she gone to the boutique's open house late, after Lily and Paul left, and hooked up with Hunter? Eve winced at the vodka's strength. "You know Adam and Paul are workout buddies?"

"He might've mentioned it." But didn't. "I didn't know Hunter—"

"—was representing Adam in a deal to build townhouses in Cherry Creek. Without his connections, the deal's dead." Eve's hand trembled on her glass. "I don't know what I'd do without him, Lily."

Lily turned to face her, forcing Eve to meet her eyes. "Hunter—or Frank?"

Eve gave a little laugh. "Adam and I saved each other, but Frank saved us both." She returned to her vodka. "A townhouse would be perfect for you and Paul. Bright and sunny—"

"Eve."

"Pittsburgh, I know." Tears welled. "I wanted to tell you, but Adam said no."

The neon aurora over the bar spun faster. Meeting Eve here, after

Hunter was killed, was nuts. But why would she or Adam sabotage CT? She had to get Adam alone.

Eve dabbed her eyes. "You'll think I'm crazy. Adam does." Does—not *is*. "We're being stalked."

The bar stopped spinning. "By whom?" Lily demanded.

"The DOJ sponsors CT because we get results. Before Pittsburgh, we did a trial run in D.C. and the Metro PD closed a dozen cold cases. Last year, Portland had similar success—" Eve did her PhD with Frank in Oregon. Was she playing her? "—but Pittsburgh was where it all began." She smiled bitterly. "He warned us this could happen."

"Frank?"

Eve quickly wiped her eyes and forced a smile. "Angela!"

What the fuck? Lily turned.

Escorted by the doorwoman and a phalanx of barmaids, Angela tapped imperiously across the floor, her steel-tipped cane ballast for a silk sheath shot with silver and gold threads. "Tonight you need friends," Eve whispered.

She knows I've been ducking Angela.

"Well, this is a cheery little crypt!" Angela boomed. "I feel like that demon doll in my library wall." Slipping the bartender a C-note, she ordered vodka and turned to Lily. "Tell me that scruffy little man at the lab has nothing to do with *Schuylerhaugh*."

"Professor Feldman?" What was she going to tell Angela? With the dioramas and murders and now Hunter dead, Benjy Schuyler's painting was the last—

"Professor, my ass," Angela snorted. "I've half a mind to call Sasha—"

"Don't!" Lily blurted.

Angela peered at her craftily. "Why not?"

I need him.

"Lily?" Angela demanded.

She'll forgive anything but a lie.

"He's supposed to be working on a project of Sasha's," Lily babbled. "She doesn't know he's in Denver."

"Then why *is*—"

In desperation, Lily knocked her elbow into Angela's drink. Vodka splashed all over her dress, making the metallic threads flash wildly in the spinning neon light.

Angela stared at her.

Tell her the truth.

The doorwoman rushed over with linen napkins. "We'll pay for dry cleaning, Ms. Kurtz—"

"No." Angela stood. "Accidents happen."

"Take it out of my pay," Lily begged.

Angela smiled kindly. "Never liked this old rag anyhow."

Eve rose. "We'll shop for a new one tomorrow after lunch." She patted Lily's arm reassuringly. "The Bistro at noon. Join us?"

Adam will be alone. "Sorry—work!" Lily said.

Angela stared at her. Lily unflinchingly met her gaze.

I'll give you Bliss Byrd's killer instead.

Chapter Twenty-Nine

"No bodies yet?" Lily asked.

Adam looked up from the Tudor diorama with a start.

"I knocked," she apologized. "Am I intruding?"

"Of course not."

In daylight, his garage studio was Santa's toyshop without the elves. An army of bendable dolls and plastic action figures peered from a shelf, and models lined the walls, some half-assembled and others awaiting final coats of stucco or paint. Adam set down his tiny brush and turned off the fan. "White noise helps me focus."

He'd been working with a jar of filling compound and a pallet of tiny bricks perfectly formed and fired from clay. Like real ones, some were redder, others pink. His new brickwork had the ingenious effect of updating the Tudor while allowing it to age gracefully.

"You got rid of the ivy!" Lily exclaimed.

Adam patted a wall tenderly. "And those nasty old pfitzers."

"You're pretty good at this."

"Just give me balsa wood, glue and an Exacto knife…. Dad had a trainset."

"A big one?"

Adam laughed. "The entire basement. He was a railroad engineer—not a real one, a front office guy. But his trains ran on time." He glanced ruefully at the titanium luxury tower. "If only buildings lived up to their models. One never seems to tell the other's story."

Lily looked more closely at the Tudor. Tearing out ivy and pfitzers weren't the only changes; since the dinner party, Adam had installed large kitchen windows and painted the exterior trim a soft green. Instead of a charmingly neglected country cottage, it was now suitable for an urban couple. Double income, no kids. *It's not a diorama until there's a victim*, she reminded herself. He seemed to read her mind.

"As usual the script's under wraps, but I told Eve to write your widower out. Now the Tudor's too nice for even a fake murder." He sighed. "A Cotswold-style cottage would never fly in Phoenix anyway."

He'd mentioned Phoenix the other night. "When's your gig?"

"Week after next." There was still time to stop it. "I told Eve to slow down, but it's been booked for months." He looked at Lily slyly. "You just missed her, by the way."

Did he know she and Eve had had drinks? Maybe one too many, but if CT really did have a stalker, Lily wanted to hear it from him. "Actually, I was looking for you."

Adam pulled a bin from the shelf. "Pick out the furniture, whatever you want, it's cheaper than Wayfair. Paintings, too—everything from Old Masters to abstracts."

"Like Hunter's?" she asked softly.

Adam took off his glasses and rubbed his eyes. Eve was right about one thing: Hunter Merritt's death had hit him hard enough to require white noise and a hod of bricks to drown it out. "How's Paul?" he asked.

"In shock." Home at two a.m., slept on the couch, gone when she'd risen. His favorite suit and tie had been balled up in the trash.

Adam nimbly sorted through some tiny trees. Bypassing a Japanese maple and flowering crabapple, he settled on a stand of spruces. "Too evergreen?"

"Adam—"

"Help me garden!" He dumped out a bin of rosebushes, perfect down to their tiny thorns. "C'mon, Lily, what'd your mom plant?" He pawed through them faster, as if everything would be fine if he finished before Christmas. But if a stalker had killed Hunter, he'd kicked the legs out from Adam's comeback for good.

"Adam, stop."

He looked up. "It's what you want, isn't it? Sun and air—"

"I want to find who killed Hunter," she said. "You do, too." His eyes widened, then he looked away. "It's happened before, and it'll happen again."

He sank into a chair. "Eve can't know."

"What makes you think she doesn't?" Lily asked.

"It'd destroy her."

Her—not CT. Lily knelt beside him. "Then make it stop."

Adam snorted. "You saw him the other night, waltzing in—"— *Frank?*—"—gets her hypnotized, thinks he owns her. What's he doing in Phoenix? He's been wiring these gigs from day one. And I introduced them!"

This wasn't making any sense.

Ping! Text from Paul. *Johnson 2day at 2.*

She turned back to Adam. "Why would Frank Gould kill three strangers?"

He shook his head. "Not them. It's *her.*"

Even less sense. "Look, Adam," Lily said firmly. "We need evidence—"—*a coherent motive*— "to give the cops. Paul has Johnson's ear, but we've got to move fast and we'd better make it good. Frank's a psych prof with a resumé a mile long."

"You've read his papers?" Adam demanded.

No Place Like Home. Lily almost laughed. If only this weren't so serious and Hunter so dead. "Facts, Adam, not psychobabble."

"Okay." He returned the landscaping materials to their bins. "It started as a lark, to keep our marriage fresh. I'd stick things in the dioramas without telling Eve. She'd do the same with the scripts. Whoever outsmarted the other—" He blushed. "Then the murders began."

"Where?" Lily asked.

"First a married couple in a Pittsburgh box. Two story, hipped roof, big porch—"

"I get the picture!"

"—identical to a CT diorama."

Coincidence.

"Next a split-level where the husband was killed. Same as a diorama, except it was a woman in ours, not a man." He put the bins back on the shelf. "It happened again in Portland, but I wasn't sure till Hunter."

Ping! Paul again. *Johnson @2.*

"I want to believe you, Adam, but—"

He folded his arms and leaned against the table. "The Pittsburgh murders were reported days after each of those dioramas went public, but the guy in the split level was killed the day *before* our training occurred. Same in Portland. We moved heaven and earth to keep those dioramas secret. Not even the cops knew."

"Cancel Phoenix," Lily said.

"I told Eve this was my last gig. I was starting to get commissions, she could afford a real miniaturist, CT had fulfilled its purpose." Adam shook his head ruefully. "She begged me to do Phoenix."

Lily thought fast. "I need addresses and dates."

"Yes, ma'am." Adam straightened, and behind his wire rims she saw the architect who'd won a Pritzker for a marvel of titanium and glass.

"And the dioramas themselves," Lily added.

Adam frowned. "We stripped D.C.'s to retrofit them." He gestured to some cruder models on a shelf. "The rest were auctioned off."

"To whom?"

He shrugged. Maybe Johnson could find out.

"One last thing," Lily said. "What does Eve know?"

Silence.

"How did Frank—" she began.

"Don't get it, do you?" Adam laughed bitterly. "They script them together."

Chapter Thirty

"Sit." Johnson had a pained look. "Please."

Lily took the chair facing his desk. He still wore yesterday's suit but his tie had a new stain. He gestured to Mr. Coffee on the credenza. The carafe was empty and the bottom was sludge. "No, thanks," she said.

Johnson raised his brows at Paul.

"Your show," Paul told him.

"Okay." Johnson's swivel chair creaked. "Ms. Sparks, I won't ask how you happened to be at the scene of *yet another*—"

"We're buying a house," Lily said.

"Mazel tov."

"Paul found Hunter, not me."

Johnson rubbed his forehead. "Let's forget the other—"

"Bruce Kemp?" she asked sweetly. "And while we're there, what leads do you have on Bliss Byrd?"

Johnson appealed mutely to Paul. Had they been talking before she arrived?

"Lily thinks the cases are connected," Paul said.

"I got that much. Ms. Sparks—"

"Let's cut the shit," she said.

Johnson winced like she was a hemorrhoid. "You first."

"CT has a stalker."

He chuckled. "Stalker?"

"The killer's copying the dioramas. You have no leads because there's no other motive. And having gotten away with it *three times*, he's unlikely—"

Johnson rocked back in his chair. "Hunter Merritt's managing partner was pretty irked at him banging his wife."

Paul shrugged innocently.

Johnson continued. "And a paralegal—excuse me, *legal assistant*—filed an EEOC complaint against him." He smiled at Lily patronizingly. "Sexual harassment. An anti-fracking mob was calling for Bruce Kemp's head on social media *and* a slew of folks lost a shitload of money when a fracking deal of his went belly-up."

Don't forget the artists whose works he flipped, Lily thought.

Johnson folded his meaty hands. "Shitload is a legal term, by the way. And by your logic, the killer's done. Three dioramas, three murders."

Got you! "Phoenix."

Johnson blinked. Lily turned just in time to catch Paul shake his head.

Where were they this weekend?

Bowles stood at the door with a guilty expression. "Lieutenant, there's an urgent call—"

Fuck this!

Lily rose. "That call can wait. Let's see the dioramas."

———

Too pissed to even look at Paul, Lily circled the table to Demi's mini-flat.

"Bliss Byrd," she said. "Realty signs, coffeemakers, cats." *Slow down.* "Tiny house, micro-studio apartment." Bowles had trailed in and nodded encouragingly. "Radical downsizing." At CT's training, what had a detective said? "No room for a man."

Bowles snickered.

"Bruce Kemp." Lily turned to Glenn's conservatory. "Glass houses—showcases. Benches and walls in an identical maze. Collectors bludgeoned or shot."

"Messy," Bowles murmured.

Johnson scowled.

Paul watched expressionlessly.

Even the shimmering turquoise water in Lance's pool seemed to mock her.

I could use some help here.

"Hunter Merritt," Lily said. "Rooftops, clubroom, clubbed…" *Don't think about the smell.* "…pool, hot tub…" *Or those sickening bits floating…* "blue, red…"

Paul winced.

She steeled herself. "…trysts, robes." She turned to Johnson. "Was Hunter clubbed?"

He grimaced. "Don't know yet."

That said it all.

"Hold on a sec," Johnson continued. Had he and Paul rehearsed this? "Assuming you're right and it's not a coincidence, which came first: the victims or the dioramas?"

Bowles fiddled nervously with the radio on his belt.

Johnson smiled smugly. "You assume the dollhouses inspired the murders, Ms. Sparks, but what if it's the other way around? What if the killer built clues from the crime scenes into the dioramas?"

She thought about the timing again. Adam had said the other murders occurred *before* the dioramas went public. "But Bruce and Hunter were killed *after*—"

Paul finally shook himself awake—or pretended to. "Johnson's right, Lily. Why assume a copycat? Cross-over clues could mean the killer was at Bruce or Hunter's houses before the dioramas were built. Or they could mean nothing."

Had she been played? She looked to Bowles for help, but he turned away.

"And why these victims?" Johnson added. "Tell me and I might take you seriously."

"I just did!" she cried.

He shook his head. "Killers don't target victims just because of a house."

Lily strode to Demi's micro-mini studio. The *For Rent* sign in front was bright blue. "You want a connection? Trudi Rood knew the houses and the victims."

Paul stared at her like she was nuts.

"That realtor gal?" Johnson guffawed. "She sells half the—"

"—and that penthouse to Hunter Merritt. Bliss Byrd's ex was his client, and he bought paintings from Bruce Kemp."

Johnson wagged his jowls. "Hunter Merritt was an art collector, so what? And a mover and shaker. Him and that la-di-da firm—sorry, Paul—probably played musical chairs with Trudi."

Lily turned to Paul. "Musical fucking chairs?"

He wouldn't meet her eyes. "Hunter's a *victim*, Lily, not—"

"I didn't say he's the killer!"

Johnson looked at Paul. *Get this woman to the psych ward.*

Lily forced herself to slow down again. "Trudi's in this up to her neck. She didn't bat an eyelash when we found Hunter dead. Maybe she was in shock, but not to ask me *a single question*—"

"But why *these* victims, Ms. Sparks?" Johnson smiled like an old cat who'd finally caught a bird. "Find me some motive for Trudi Rood to kill three people in order to destroy Castle Training, and we'll talk."

Paul had left his roost by the wall. Now he gave her a little hug. "This isn't personal."

"Personal?"

"You're trying too hard, Lily." He kissed her cheek. "I'll be back tomorrow night."

"What?" she said.

"Flight to catch. Hunter's case."

"Where?"

He kissed her again.

"Get some sleep. We'll go to dinner when I get back."

—

Johnson couldn't be right. Not just about motive, but anything.

At the first stoplight, Lily pulled out her phone. No message from Angela. She didn't want to think what that meant; she was too keyed up and furious to think at all. As for Paul— *Fuck dinner!*

If Johnson was right, and the killer had access to the victims' houses before the dioramas were built, it didn't matter when they were murdered. Bliss Byrd was easy—her house was plastered all over YouTube.

Horns tooted.

She tried Raf at the lab. No answer.

If Johnson was right, the killer had been in Hunter Merritt's clubroom and at Bruce Kemp's soirée. The Castles attended art events; Michel and Gina had paved their way. Did they bring Adam and Eve to Bruce's? Eve was supposed to be at Paul's open house too. If she arrived later, maybe Hunter invited her to his clubroom.

She texted Eve. *Dropped by 2day + missed U.*

No reply.

Paul was tight with Adam, and in the bag with Johnson. Raf was AWOL. This was up to her. She stared at her phone, willing it to ping. Did the murder scenes inspire the dioramas, or were the dioramas roadmaps for the killer? Or was he a copycat who targeted victims because of something their houses said? No matter what, he had to be neck-deep in CT. She tapped some keys.

Frank Gould + DU.

His final lecture was tonight.

Chapter Thirty-One

Lecture-goers lined the auditorium steps, early birds leaned forward in their seats, and coeds perched cross-legged at the foot of the dais. As Frank Gould paced the stage under the hot lights, his hair shone like a helmet. He'd canned the deferential stoop from the Castles' dinner party; now his powerful shoulders filled his jacket like a dress uniform. On his chest something glimmered. A medal? No, the lapel mic, or a silver curl peeking from the top button of his burgundy silk shirt. Lily pictured Eve in his arms.

Arriving half an hour late, she'd been lucky to find a parking space. Parking was always tough around DU, with the sports arenas and college bars, but this crowd wasn't just students. Many were older, and all were rapt. Looking down from the rear of the darkened auditorium, Lily didn't see a single cell screen lit. Suddenly Frank stopped pacing and turned. Impossible as it was, his eyes seemed to find hers. His voice rang out.

"Under the cruelest conditions, what sustains us?"

A man in front of Lily shifted. Like a butterfly flapping its wings, the minute gesture cascaded. A woman in the aisle below grabbed the railing, and Lily had to restrain herself from reaching for the boy next to her. The auditorium was stuffy, and she'd had no time for lunch.

Frank resumed pacing. "In captivity, we create it…"

Focus. To the Castles, the dioramas were a game. Adam planted Demi's cat, and Eve missed its significance and the bludgeon that killed Lance. In their own little domestic drama, who kept score?

The man in front of Lily swayed again, and a wave of nausea hit her. She surveyed the darkened chamber. Half-way down and dead center was an empty seat. She slipped down the aisle, steadying herself on the handrail as she went. "Sorry," she whispered as those in the row glared and scooted over. Breathing heavily, she sank into the seat. The woman next to her was too rapt to notice.

Eve Castle.

"… primal need for the sanctuary we call home," Frank ended.

Eve slowly exhaled.

"Eve?" Lily said.

Still fixated on Frank, Eve rose and clapped. The auditorium erupted in applause. Fire and safety codes be damned: DU had a hit. A flushed administrator stepped to the podium and grinned playfully. "Next time we'll book the Ball Arena for Professor Gould! Perhaps sooner than you think." She turned to Frank. "Time for a question or two?"

The audience settled back. In the first row, a scholarly gent creakily rose. "Professor Gould, could you expand on your research into POWs? Specifically, who best survives captivity and torture?"

Frank smiled. "As you know, James—"—knowing chuckles from the audience— "there's two schools of thought on who makes it home. Some say optimists, because they never lose hope. But false hope is cruel. To break someone, raise their hope of returning home and then destroy it inch by inch. Ask a man on death row if execution's kinder."

"How bleak!" James cried.

Frank ducked his head impishly. The audience laughed.

"Answer the question, Frank," James chided. "Who survives?"

Eve leaned forward.

"Pessimists, of course." Frank left the podium and stood before the audience. "Not by building castles in the air, but by imagining the worst." Whispers and shifting in seats. "Dorothy fetishizes Kansas, but you don't have to be swept up in a tornado to pine for an illusion."

The crowd fell silent.

"Home, of course, can be anywhere or nowhere," Frank continued. "It's what you make of it. But instead of fantasizing about a sanctuary that never was, wouldn't we be better off preparing for life without it?"

"Come now, Frank," James insisted. "If not nostalgia for home, something must keep us going. I believe your research with former POWs led you to a controversial conclusion."

The chuckles this time were nervous, and there was no humor in Frank's smile. "What sustained the men I interviewed was rage and a desire for revenge." Gasps from the audience. "So much for the green, green grass of home."

The DU woman smoothly stepped to the podium. "I believe Professor Gould has dinner planned somewhere west of Topeka. On that note—"

James' voice rose. "You're saying home doesn't exist?"

Frank shrugged. "Why assume we're meant to be safe? Let's agree on a new definition, James. One you might find more... *hopeful*. However tiny our universe, it's human nature to try to harness it and make it obey."

A boy waved. "If I'm a POW, can I make my captors obey, too?"

Frank reared back, then grinned. "If I told you how, I'd have to kill you."

James led the final laughter and the applause.

Chapter Thirty-Two

The lights came on.

"Terrific talk!" Lily said.

Eve blinked like she'd woken from a spell. "I didn't see you."

"I'm kicking myself for coming late. What'd I miss?"

Eve regained her poise. "He was brilliant."

People were flocking to Frank. The DU administrator beamed and a woman in a tuxedo cut through the crowd to pump his hand. "Did he say anything about houses mirroring psyches?" Lily asked.

Eve laughed. "Dinner talk."

"But there's peer-reviewed research?" Lily said.

Eve smiled ruefully. "Publish or perish." Seats around them emptied but she was still watching the stage. "Frank pushes the envelope, but a theory's only good if you can test it. He has an idea for taking CT to the next level.... Where's Paul?"

"Stepping in for Hunter at the firm," Lily replied.

Eve finally turned. "Trouble in paradise?"

"Not really."

Eve patted her hand. "The condo's yours, not his. Once you find a place together, you'll miss the good old days!" Under the harsh light, her face suddenly sagged. "Adam says you dropped by."

"We talked about Hunter." And Frank.

"Whatever it was, I'm grateful," Eve said. "Adam hasn't been so motivated and... *purposeful* since..." She trailed off. "We'll take you house-hunting."

"But Trudi Rood—"

"Did she show you anything you liked?" Eve asked.

"Not yet," Lily admitted.

"Adam has something specific in mind," Eve insisted. "When does Paul get back?"

"Tomorrow evening."

"We won't take long, just drive by." Alone onstage at last, Frank was fussing with his lapel mic. Eve patted her hair.

"Shall we meet you and Adam at six?" Lily asked.

Frank glanced up, and Eve stirred. Lily touched her gently on the arm.

"What?" Eve said.

"The house tour."

"Of course," Eve replied.

Frank stepped into the well of the auditorium.

"Do you agree with him?" Lily asked.

"About home?" Eve laughed softly. "Oz, Kansas—we all have somewhere we're running to or from."

"DU is wooing him." Lily squeezed Eve's hand. "See you tomorrow night."

She snuck out as Frank mounted the steps.

———

Lily knew who Eve was running to. But what was Adam running from?

She gave Jack extra kibble and turned on her laptop.

Clicking to CT's launch in *The Pittsburgh Gazette*, she skipped the photo spread and reread the story. It wasn't just local boy made good; the launch had been a homecoming of sorts for Eve, too. Her psychology practice began there. How far back did she and Trudi Rood go? A diorama of a split-level with a woman face down on the floor caught Lily's eye. It was striking how CT's dioramas had evolved.

She scrolled to a black-and-white photograph of a boy with glasses and knobby knees sitting on a doorstep. The house itself seemed dwarfed by a powerfully built man in a short-sleeved dress shirt with pens in his pocket and a ridiculously wide tie. *Adam and Ed Castle 1984*, the caption read. What had Adam said? *Those trains ran on time.* Then the Pritzker Prize medallion and Adam toasting Eve at CT's Pittsburgh launch. The adult Adam looked even less like his dad, but as he toasted his wife his smile seemed genuine and the eyes behind the wire rims brimmed with happiness. At least one of Frank Gould's domestic ideas had worked. Lily turned off her computer and switched on the TV.

Jack jumped up. Disdainfully turning his back on the screen, he began licking his rump. Flat images never fooled him; unlike humans, he had no trouble differentiating reality from a representation. Maybe the dioramas were nothing more than that. Lily thought of the photos in *The Gazette*'s spread. The story's hook was local boy makes good; why no recent shot of proud dad Ed? She re-opened her laptop.

Ed Castle.

1986 obit. Lily closed the laptop. Wherever Paul was, it was too late for him to call. She switched off her lamp. With her full attention at last, Jack curled up. She reached for her computer again.

Ed Castle + obit.

The short paragraph identified Ed as a twenty-year employee of the Pittsburgh & Lake Erie Railroad and his wife Mary as a homemaker. No information as to how and when either of them had died, but the obit gave their address. Public records said Adam's childhood home had been razed in 1986, around the time of the obit, and Google Earth showed rubble and grass. Lily returned to the property records. In 1976, the Castles had bought their house from Thomas and Margery Brown.

Thomas + Margery + Brown.

Nothing on Tom, but Marge was an active volunteer—a plump, motherly-looking woman presiding over a bake sale for local fire fighters.

Thomas + Margery Brown + 1975.

Jackpot: the newlywed Browns posed proudly in front of their first home.

Of course.

A Tudor with a brick façade, a stone chimney and pfitzers lining the front walk.

Chapter Thirty-Three

The Ford Taurus had light bars on the grill and a spotlight next to the driver's side mirror. As it glided to the curb at PDX's arrival pick-up site, the plainclothes cop at the wheel recognized Paul, too.

"Agent Reilly?" he said. Professional courtesy, or Paul's DOJ contact hadn't informed the Portland cops he was no longer with the FBI.

"Paul," he replied.

"Niall." College kid, if not for the clipped tone and hair, and biceps that didn't come from eating granola. He eyed Paul's nylon briefcase. "Luggage?"

Paul tossed the bag with his fresh shirt and skivvies in the Taurus' backseat. "Just overnight."

"Where to?" Niall asked.

"Let's grab a beer."

———

At the college dive, the barkeep gave Paul the once-over, but in a black T-shirt and jeans Niall fit right in. Paul paid for their craft ales and brought them to a booth. "Hope I'm not blowing your cover."

Niall laughed. "Half these guys are feds. Punk bars are where the real action is."

Paul raised his glass. "To grunge." The ale was surprisingly good. "You were at CT's diorama training here last year."

Niall shrugged. "A cut above the usual DOJ dog and pony show, but not real useful for undercover." Paul followed his eyes to a kid slipping something to the bartender. "Weed," Niall muttered. "Like I said, punk bars are more fun." He signaled for another round of beer.

"CT," Paul prompted. "What do you remember?"

"The dioramas were slick."

"Any one in particular?" There'd been no pictures of Portland's dioramas on the web.

Niall shook his head. "CT was still working out kinks."

"Kinks?" The second-round brew showed off its hops.

"The presenter kept tipping us off," Niall replied.

Paul nodded. "Kind of defeats the purpose."

"Yeah—a defense lawyer would have a field day with him."

Maybe he'd misheard. "You mean her," Paul said.

"Nope," Niall insisted, "a guy."

"Sandy-haired, glasses?"

"Nah." Niall shook his head emphatically. "Adam Castle stood in back. The other guy was the trainer."

Third guess. "Frank Gould?"

"Yeah! That shrink from Eugene."

From DARPA to Tulane to the University of Oregon. And now on to Phoenix.

"Are you up for a drive tomorrow?" Paul asked.

—

Niall swung by Paul's hotel early. "We're making a stop."

"Where?" Paul asked. His appointment with Gould's former colleague in Eugene was at ten a.m.

"You asked about cold cases," Niall replied. "This one's freaky, lots of press."

"Two years ago?"

"A week after the dioramas."

"But Eugene's a hundred miles—"

"We'll make it in time." Niall revved the Taurus and grinned. "This ride's hotter than the piece of shit you probably drive, and I ain't getting a ticket."

—

The Portland suburb was on a lake surrounded by magnificent pines and multi-million-dollar houses. Niall's crime scene was two stacks of concrete and glass linked by a suspension bridge and softened by a stand of Japanese maples. There was a private pier, but no *For Sale* sign. The eerie isolation reminded Paul of the Pittsburgh Foursquare where that couple had been murdered.

"Where is everyone?" he asked.

"They've dropped the price three times," Niall said.

Maybe the killer has a thing against realtors, Paul thought irreverently. "Was the crime scene messy?"

"No." Niall laughed. "It's a smart house."

"Show me."

The house was a model of environmentalism and sustainability. Triple-glazed sliding glass doors, geothermal heat pumps, a rainwater-recovery system. In a nod to the lake, the stairways inside the cubes floated. Paul kept looking for signs of a crime, but the slate floors were as blank as the walls. "What happened?"

"Leo Tilson was a tech entrepreneur. He died from antifreeze poisoning."

"Sounds like an accident," Paul said.

Niall shrugged. "We looked into a leak in the closed-loop geothermal system."

"And?"

"The house didn't kill him. And his dog was okay."

"Dog?" Paul asked.

"Antifreeze tastes sweet."

"Still—"

Niall shook his head. "Nobody ingests antifreeze by accident."

"Suicide?"

"Damn rare, and Leo's company was about to go public." Niall locked up. "He had dinner at a local spot but could've gone bar-hopping later in Portland. Leo liked Blue Margaritas, and everyone liked Leo."

"Women or guys?"

"Either or both," Niall said, "but someone had a hard-on for him. It took two days for Leo to die."

Nothing added up. "Didn't he try to get help?"

"Called in sick to his CFO and said he'd had a bad oyster."

They climbed back in the Taurus. "How far is the ER?" Paul asked.

"One mile." Niall snapped his fingers. "Oh, I forgot. Leo's Porsche Cayenne Turbo S's tires were slashed and the power to the house was cut. But someone was considerate enough to let his dog out."

"An animal rights activist?" Paul asked doubtfully.

Niall gunned the Taurus. "We don't want to become another San Francisco or Seattle."

"Eco-terrorist?" Even more unlikely.

"Installing a geothermal pump and driving a hybrid Porsche doesn't fool anyone," Niall said spiritedly. "But what killing another sorry-ass tech entrepreneur has to do with dioramas, you tell me."

They did 90 mph all the way to Eugene without being stopped.

—

Carl Peters had a neat beard, a sardonic smile and excellent coffee. They drank it in his office in the University of Oregon's psych department in a brick building at the center of campus. Carl didn't ask why they were interested in his former colleague. Maybe he was used to being questioned about Frank.

"He got a bum rap," Carl said.

"How?" Paul asked.

"A student outed him."

Niall leaned forward. "Coed?"

"We were all young once." Carl laughed. "Frank's weakness isn't girls, it's ideas. Luring him from Tulane was quite a 'get'. He's spellbinding in the classroom and PhD candidates vied for him to be their advisor."

"So what happened?" Paul asked.

"Some J-school kid got ahold of a paper Frank wrote when he was a young Turk at DOD, and splattered it all over *The Daily Emerald*. Frank's piece was highly theoretical—I'm sure he's embarrassed by it now. The government loves to throw money at crazy theories."

"What theory?" Niall demanded.

"Frank's?" Carl seemed amused. "Under times of stress, we seek safety."

"A pub!" Niall snorted.

"Try putting it in the context of torture victims," Carl said. "The military's a flashpoint; any whiff of using soldiers or POWs as lab rats is controversial. At a public university like ours, Frank was caught in the crosshairs."

"There must be more," Paul insisted.

"It was Frank's definition of safety," Carl admitted. "According to him, instead of finding strength in a fantasized sanctuary, his subjects survived by projecting their rage against their parents onto their captors."

Niall whistled. "No shit!"

"It incited an avalanche of criticism from all sides," Carl continued, "and there were questions about how Frank conducted his interviews. But like a good spook, he refused to discuss his research. There was some noise about the American Psychological Association getting involved, but they wisely stayed out."

Paul still wasn't buying it. "And that's why Frank left?"

Carl busied himself with his coffee. "Not quite."

Niall leaned in. "So it was a girl."

"Grad student," Carl reluctantly admitted. "Consensual, apparently…"

Eve Castle?

"...and maddeningly confidential. Somebody filed an anonymous complaint. "

Score one for Adam Castle. Paul glanced at his watch and started to rise.

"So what?" Niall demanded. "Prof that popular—"

"Don't worry about Frank," Carl assured him. "A desert with a golf course is his nirvana. Arizona was lucky to get him, and so will DU."

"DU?" Paul said.

"Or wherever he goes next." Carl winked. "Frank's quite... *popular*."

Chapter Thirty-Four

Raf looked over Lily's shoulder at the computer screen.

Trudi Rood + Pittsburgh.

No hits.

"Eve said the copycat crimes began there," Lily explained. Stalking seemed increasingly farfetched. "Maybe she and Trudi knew each other."

Raf shook his head doubtfully. "She seemed surprised when Trudi said she was a Steel City gal."

"Maybe there's a connection Eve doesn't know."

Raf left her and ambled towards *Schuylerhaugh*. "I love a good obsession, Lily, but shouldn't we be figuring out what to tell Angela?"

"I know, I know…" Trudi + realtor + Steel City. A group shot in a convention hall showed a younger Trudi with big teeth. "At the National Realtors Conference and Expo in Pittsburgh, she was Trudi Pryor."

"Hah!" Raf came back to the computer. "I knew Rood wasn't her real name."

Trudi Pryor + Frank Gould.

Raf frowned. "Frank?"

"Longshot," Lily admitted.

Pryor + Eve Castle.

"Seriously, Lily. The Rensselaer's—"

Commonwealth v. Pryor. "Bingo!" Lily skimmed the Pennsylvania appellate court opinion. "Thomas Michael Pryor was convicted of sexual assault on a child, and Eve was the boy's therapist. They affirmed the conviction but raked Eve over the coals for calling the male doll Tommy." She looked up at Raf. "This must be why she closed her practice."

"Yeah, maybe. So?"

"She lied about it, Raf!" Lily said triumphantly. "What if Trudi and Tommy are related? They're about the right age to be brother and sister. There's your big simple value pattern: Trudi brings CT down to punish Eve for sending her brother up the river."

Raf frowned. "Tommy loses his appeal, so Trudi kills three random strangers?"

"Not random, Raf!" she insisted. "Maybe Trudi's victims were stand-ins for CT's diorama dolls. Poetic justice, given what Eve did to her brother."

He shook his head. "Even if they're related, there's a gaping hole in your pattern: *why them?*" First Johnson, now him. "You don't kill three strangers just because you're pissed at someone else. If Trudi's only connection to the victims is selling them their houses—"

"She combs the obits for listings, Raf!"

He snorted. "Jesus, Lily, there's a world of difference between getting the jump on new properties and planting their owners in the ground. Face it, you're barking up the wrong tree. If the dioramas and the murders are related, we need someone with a grudge against the Castles, Bliss Byrd, Bruce Kemp, *and* Hunter Merritt…"

A furious staccato made them look up.

"Why isn't that in a crate on its way to Albany?" Angela thundered across the floor. She thumped her way over and waved a certificate in Lily's face. "You know how much the Rensselaer paid to insure a Cole?" She focused on Raf. "What's he still doing here?"

"Angela—" Lily began.

"Never mind." Angela's stick pounded the floor. "Professor Feldman, my ass."

"The PhD's real," he replied mildly.

"I know who you are." Angela turned back to Lily. "I expect nothing of him, but *you*—You think Sasha and I don't talk? You lied to me!"

Lily looked at Raf.

Impassively he gazed back. *What keeps you honest?*

Slowly she exhaled.

"I lied," she admitted. It was such a relief to say it.

"Why?" Angela demanded.

"I'm in over my head." That felt pretty damn good, too. Not perfect— but good.

"Fine." Angela's scorn seared. "Now that you're no longer *drowning*—"

Lily stood her ground. We can't send *Schuylerhaugh* out."

Angela's steel-tipped stick ratatated across the tile floor. She raised it and pointed it at the canvas. With the delicacy of a wolverine's snout, the tip probed the paint. A salmon-colored particle wended to her feet. "Use the Tate's stretcher bars!"

Lily shook her head.

"What'll I tell Benjy?" Angela demanded.

The molting paused.

"That it's not a real Cole," Lily said.

Angela's response was clipped. "How much is the Kurtz Foundation paying for my father's oldest friend's legacy to be slandered and demeaned?"

"Not a cent," Lily replied. "I paid Raf's airfare from my pocket."

The cane thumped. Paint rained down from *Schuylerhaugh*'s sky, opening another patch of white. "Professor Feldman will be lucky if he ever finds another job in the art world!"

The lab pulsed. Lily looked again at Raf.

What kind of lab do you want to run? his look said.

"If he goes," Lily said, "so do I."

Raf's jaw dropped.

"For a lousy Cole?" Angela sputtered.

Fuck it. "I'll e-mail you my resignation."

"Don't waste my time," Angela spat.

Leaving a salmon drift in her wake, she stomped out.

—

Raf applauded. "Nice job! You'll like McDonald's joe."

Lily sank in her chair. "I thought you'd appreciate my loyalty."

He nodded in admiration. "I do."

"Are you this bad an influence on everyone?" she asked.

"Hopefully."

In an hour Paul landed, and they were supposed to go house-hunting with the Castles. Her career was over. Gina and Michel would break out petits fours and champagne. "Shit," Lily said. "What'll I tell him?"

"Your FBI guy?" Raf scoffed. "That ship's sailed."

"Thanks."

"If you haven't driven him away yet, I doubt this will."

Her gaze swept the lab. She'd just gotten the hang of the Leica and the electric easel. She'd even mastered the fucking espresso machine. This had started to feel like home.

But Raf was surprisingly chipper. "What's our next move, boss?"

"Move?" she said bleakly.

"With *Schuylerhaugh* squared away, your calendar's clear. Want some help with those murders?"

Chapter Thirty-Five

Lily stared at the McMansion from the curb. The slate-roofed stucco had stone reliefs with fleurs de lis, but tonight not even a real Mediterranean villa could tempt her.

"What's wrong with this one, Lily?" Paul said testily.

The Castles exchanged a glance.

"Magnificent firs and elms!" Eve exclaimed.

"The corner means just two neighbors," Adam coaxed, "and the setback mutes traffic." He was beginning to sound like Trudi Rood. They'd stopped at a dozen places with *For Sale* signs but skipped over the Tiffany blue *TR*'s. "Japanese garden tucked to the side..."

Lily looked at Paul. He'd been very quiet since he landed; Hunter's death must have hit him even harder than she'd thought. And when they ditched the Castles, she'd have to deliver more bad news.

Now he forced a smile. "This one's too big, that was too small. Goldilocks here—"

Lily tried to sound reasonable. "That carriage house was a fixer-upper, Paul."

"What's wrong with that?" he demanded.

"For a guy who can't change a lightbulb—" She stopped herself. It wasn't Paul's fault she'd lost her job.

"I just want a garage," he said through gritted teeth.

"You'd put an offer on the City Dump to get this over with!" she cried.

"Now, dear," Eve soothed. She signaled Adam, who slung his arm over Paul's shoulders and led him around the corner and up the street. "He'd do anything to please you."

"I know," Lily said.

"Then what's wrong?"

I have to tell him my career is over. "Nothing."

"Is it the commitment, or fear of ending up where you left? A house is a blank slate, Lily. Home is—"

"Yeah, I know. What you make it."

Frank Gould. Talk about Dorothy pining for Oz. She'd chased a rabbit down a hole, taken a detour to Never-Never land, played a costly game of house. Raf and Johnson were right: No killer had four completely unrelated grudges. Bliss Byrd's death was an accident like Demi's. Bruce Kemp was killed in a home invasion or because he'd lost someone a boatload of money. Hunter Merritt couldn't keep it in his pants. The real object lesson was that her perfect eye didn't always work.

"Let's call it a night," Adam said.

"Great idea," Paul replied.

Eve gave Adam her keys and climbed in the backseat with Lily. *No domestic bloodshed in the Mercedes, please!* In silence, they motored down the leafy parkway. At another Tiffany blue sign, Adam sniffed. Suddenly he hit the brakes. "Hel-*lo*. How'd we miss this?" There was no *For Sale* sign, but the place looked empty. They must have driven past earlier because of the *TR* next door. "Needs a little work, but that's easily handled."

"Not too big or small," Eve said.

"Just right," Adam agreed.

Lily peered past Paul. The house was on a generous lot. The stately walk curved to a cottage with a stone chimney, and the setting sun stained the Virginia Creeper on the wall red. She pictured worn linoleum and claustrophobic rooms. Dad's bungalow—or Adam's Tudor? "It's late," she said.

The Castles exchanged a look.

"Last stop," Adam promised.

Eve nodded again.

They planned this. "I'm really tired," Lily said apologetically, "and Paul just landed—"

Paul exited the car and smiled grimly.

Without victims, Adam's Tudor was incomplete.

Thunder rumbled. Heat—no rain.

"C'mon, Lily," Paul said tightly. She'd pushed him into this, too. "Adam and Eve have put themselves out for us. Be a sport."

"You go," she said. "I'll wait."

He opened her door.

Chapter Thirty-Six

Lily followed Adam up the walk. "You planned this."

He poked her playfully. "Tear out the creeper and plant hydrangeas."

"You know I hate Tudors!" she said. "How could you do this?"

"Drove by and Googled the address," he replied innocently. "The owners were a rheumatologist and his wife. She died last year and he went in June. I spoke to the heirs."

"I'm surprised you don't scour obits."

"A Trudi Rood move," he scoffed. She wasn't going down that rabbit hole again. "And there wasn't an obit. This is one of the last un-redeveloped sites on the parkway, and they didn't want a flood of offers. But it's perfect for you and Paul." He winked. "Admit it, you're dying to look inside."

The gables and pitched roof had an enticing gingerbread effect. Casement windows with diamond-shaped glass lent dignity, and the chimney was enormous. Lily pictured an elderly physician and his wife at the fireside. An east-facing ell had been added. Breakfast nook?

"Heinz 57 style," Paul remarked.

"Piecemeal construction adds charm," Adam said. "Each family leaves its mark."

Shriveled coleuses were in stone urns flanking the door. Adam reached under an urn for the key. When he unlocked the door, the odors of meatloaf and old socks assailed them. "I'll turn on the AC," he said quickly.

The interior walls were textured plaster, the staircase was stained oak, and the ceiling beams were timbered. The fireplace took up most of a wall, and a chandelier appeared to be made from the antlers of a trophy moose. Lily began to feel a certain dread.

"I always wanted a fireplace," Paul said.

Adam peered under the grate. "You'll need new logs, but there's an igniter. No futzing with newspaper or candle wax and dryer lint, just a butane lighter." A flat-headed key protruded from a valve in the wall. "We'll get the gas line inspected."

Eve was already in the kitchen. "Lily, look!"

Greyish film covered the stained glass over the sink. The slate floor might as well be linoleum. Lily heard the doctor's defeated step.

"We'll get a cleaning crew," Adam promised.

"Look at these spices!" Eve peered at a lazy Susan. The brands hadn't been in grocery stores in years. A can of wax beans with a peeling label and a dented box of cake mix were in the cabinet above the sink.

Get me out of here.

"Paul—" But he and Adam had proceeded to the dining room. The walnut hutch held a set of Franciscan ware. Instead of apples like Mom's, the pattern was roses. The heavy-footed table was nothing like scarred Formica. "Let's go."

"What?" Paul said. "It's everything you want, Lily. Yard, sunlight, air…"

A tomb.

"She doesn't like the furniture," Adam said shrewdly, "and we can knock out the wall to the kitchen. Use your eye, Lily, should that footstool and chair be closer to the hearth?"

Help you finish the diorama. Lily took Paul's arm firmly. "We're going now."

Adam laughed. "A house is just a shell, Lily. The kitchen fills with the aroma of cookies baking, or the crash of dishes hurled in a sink. At the table, Dad asks how school was or retreats to his paper while you—"

Eve interrupted softly. "We get the picture, Adam."

"Do you?" His wire-rims flashed. "Why do you think I build your dioramas, Eve, so the people in them end up dead? It's to make things come out right!"

He'd better knock off Frank... We should've stuck with Trudi... Get me out of here!

Paul squeezed her hand. "Okay if we talk it over, Eve, and get back to you tomorrow?"

"Of course!" She looked relieved.

Adam turned off the AC and jiggled the door behind them to make sure it locked. The porch light came on. "Phoenix," he whispered to Lily conspiratorially. "I'll install a motion detector in my Tudor along with that fireplace."

Eve gave Lily an affectionate squeeze. "Rough day tomorrow?" she asked.

Raf would fly home. Angela would get her resignation letter. She had to face Paul.... Adam returned the key to the urn. As he rose, the light caught his smirk.

Their eyes locked.

"You don't need a fireplace in Phoenix," Lily said.

"Oh?" He winked. "Welcome home."

Chapter Thirty-Seven

"We need to talk," Lily said.

"No shit!" Paul was furious. "I can't change a lightbulb?"

"I didn't mean that."

"Really?" Tires squealed as he turned into the park. "Who was that mutt in your lab?"

"I lost my job, Paul."

"What the *fuck*?" Paul slammed the brakes and parked. "Angela fired you?"

"I quit."

Paul closed his eyes and shook his head. "Me, too."

This was going sideways. "You're wiped out, Paul. Let's talk in the morning."

"You never meant us to buy a place, did you?" he said.

"Not that Tudor."

He turned to look at her. "Tudor?" he said derisively. "You never left your Dad's frigging bungalow!" His eyes burned. "So what if your parents were miserable there? You're not your Mom and I'm sure as hell not him."

"Paul—" She reached for his hand.

He yanked it back. "You never believed we had a future."

"You're the one who keeps jumping on a plane!" she shouted.

He started the car. "One of us has to keep a job."

"It's been a shitty day. Let's go home."

"Home?" Paul laughed. "Where there's no room for me?" He drove to the condo and pulled into the loading zone. "I don't give a fuck about that mutt in the lab, Lily, but what's with you and Eve?"

"Eve?" Now she almost laughed.

"Shrinks become therapists to deal with their own shit, Lily."

"Adam stood by her when it counted."

"Yeah? Was that before or after Frank Gould?" Paul shook his head. "Come on, honey. Pfitzers, dragging us to a musty old place you're sure to hate? I'm telling you, the Castles are screwing with our heads."

"That's crazy—" she began.

"Who makes miniature crime scenes because a DARPA spook tells them to?" he demanded.

"DARPA?" Lily asked incredulously.

Paul stared out the windshield. "Trust me.'"

"Trust?" she sputtered. "Where were you yesterday and last weekend?" His silence said her flailing accusation had hit the mark. "At least lie to my face!"

Paul's grip tightened on the wheel. "I told you, Hunter—"

She flung open her door. "If the Castles are getting into anyone's head, it's yours!"

—

Lily stomped around the condo, gathering Paul's things and shoving them in his bag. Wherever he'd gone, he hadn't taken his overnighter. And last weekend—was it a coincidence Johnson had signed out too? She threw Paul's shaving gear in his dop kit—amazing how big the counter instantly was!—ignoring the sandalwood wafting from his brush. When was the last time he'd traveled without it? Paul resorting to a disposable razor almost made her laugh. Almost. Where had he been?

Sure, he resented Eve and Raf; she'd had no time for him. That new firm, guys making passes at anyone who walked in the door. What a dreadful place. He was the new kid on the block and with Hunter gone… She reached for her phone but stopped just in time. He was holding out on her. DARPA—Frank's ex-employer. Big deal. But was it?

No place like home.

She'd had it with ex-spooks.

Ask a man on death row if execution's kinder.

Please.

You never left that frigging bungalow, Paul said.

But Frank was wrong about one thing: where you lived didn't have a damn thing to do with how you ended up. Dad's bungalow wasn't to blame for Mom leaving. It was miserable because her parents were unhappy, not the other way around.

She yanked Paul's ties from the rack and threw them in the bag. A faint scent of clove wafted up. Didn't care about his suits, did he? She threw them in too. Incredible how much more space there was in the closet—why, it was almost as big as Demi's! But the clove made her eyes well. She dropped his suitcase and sank on it. He was everywhere.

Her phone pinged. Not him. Trudi Rood.

Lily flung the phone on the bed.

She pictured Paul that day twelve years ago, when she'd first laid eyes on him. His broad shoulders filling the doorway of her senior partner's office. The sudden jolt of recognition in his eyes. The way he looked at her—a little foolish, a little stunned—told her everything about how he felt. The man she loved more than anything in the world.

Lights in the high rises across the park were winking out.

She gave in and bawled.

When Lily looked up again, all but the last row of lights were extinguished.

That frigging bungalow is history.

Jack jumped up beside her.

She blew her nose and gave him a rub. Then she went to the kitchen and turned on the kettle.

She'd lied to Angela. She'd lost her job and maybe Paul. But the murders called out in a familiar voice. *What do you see, Lily?* Dad's game had taught her to find order and patterns when there seemed to be none. She poured the tea.

Staring into her cup, she visualized Raf. His daily object lessons, drawing a sphere or cylinder or block, then lighting and shading them until they rose like magic from the page. *Drawing is a miracle*, she heard him say, *to make something from nothing.* Tearing out the page, crumpling it up, tossing it in the trash. Over and over, until the lessons added up to something big. The details that completed the picture. Now she pictured the dioramas.

They were sly—ironic. Girl reaching for law book, her climb up the ladder cut short by downsizing of the most radical sort. Bonsai cultivator slain at the altar of his prized specimen. BMW manager a victim not of a rooftop poolside tryst, but a stranger from the Airbnb next door. But a big simple value pattern? Sorry, Raf.

Lily finished her tea and rinsed the cup. Then she unpacked Paul's bag and hung up his suits and ties. They really didn't take much room; the closet actually felt bigger with them. She put his shaving gear back on the counter by the sink where it belonged. She washed her face and looked in the mirror. Same crow's feet, new lines around her mouth. Big simple value pattern?

Home wasn't this condo. It was him.

She turned off the light. Once again, she pictured the crime scenes.

Bliss Byrd's tiny house. Geraniums in the windows, little red door. Interior tidy, everything in its place. No room for a man. Bruce Kemp's Modernist gas station with the cantilevered roof. Glass showcase inviting—*daring*—the world to watch him destroy young artists as he pumped up their prices and flooded the secondary market with their work. Hunter Merritt's rooftop clubroom. His hot tub the hunting ground where the hunter himself was clubbed.

Paul would have a field day with this. God, she wished he were here!

But the object lessons added up to a simple suspect.

Adam Castle.

Eve had no room for him. To recoup their investment in his dream, his Miami backers were flooding the market with unsold luxury units. Did he catch Hunter and Eve together in that penthouse clubroom? Instead of templates, maybe the dioramas were confessions.

Lily turned out the light and climbed into bed.

A confession was an invitation.

Game on: Phoenix.

Chapter Thirty-Eight

"Slept well?" Paul asked. He had a nick under his ear, and his suit looked like he'd steamed it in the shower.

"We both needed it," Lily said.

The waiter served their eggs. Paul doused his with so much pepper and tabasco they looked like a car accident. "Shouldn't you be at work?" he said. "Oh, I forgot!"

"That's mean."

He shoveled some eggs. "Was it the mutt, or *Schuylerhaugh*?"

"I lied to Angela."

Paul set down his fork. "An apology's a start."

The waiter refilled their coffee.

"It's complicated," Lily replied.

"Yeah? Lies are simple." Paul dumped on more tabasco. "Promises, too."

She flushed. "I want us to buy a house. But if you keep walking out—"

"Okay, okay." He pushed aside the eggs. "Start at the beginning."

She told him about Raf and *Schuylerhaugh*.

"Give Angela credit," Paul said. "George Kurtz may have laundered fakes, but she's not her father. Now about these murders. Johnson—"

"Why hasn't he arrested Adam?" she demanded.

"For building dollhouses?" Paul scoffed. "His only crime is loving his wife. But steer clear."

"Of Eve?" Lily laughed. "Her crime is worshipping Frank."

The waiter silently whisked away the tortured eggs. "Prima donna," Paul muttered. He stared into his coffee.

"What?" Lily said. "A lead?"

He sighed. "Frank Gould."

"Why on earth—"

"Adam cost him tenure in Oregon," Paul said. "Why would he talk the Castles into starting CT?"

"To save their marriage." That sounded stupid now.

"Or frame Adam…"

"By *murdering* people?" she replied.

Frank was a prof with a roving eye and a gold-plated CV. The academy's esteem for him was obvious at the lecture at DU. And what was so controversial about what he said? Home was an abstraction; it existed but didn't. Like her law professors' gobbledygook, his provocativeness was designed to make you think. She tried to signal the waiter to bring Paul a fresh plate of eggs.

"There's stuff about Frank you don't know," Paul said.

"Crackpot ideas and his military career?" she scoffed.

"It's classified, but Frank knows torture."

The waiter slid by and contemptuously dropped the check. Paul gave him a generous tip.

"Coming home tonight?" Lily said brightly.

Paul pushed back his chair. "After tomorrow, I swear."

She bit her tongue. "Where to now?"

"Believe it or not, Hunter had real clients. And one of us needs a job." He leaned down and kissed her on the lips. "Johnson and I are on it. We'll get the killer, but I want a promise in return."

"Stay away from Eve?" she sniped.

"And the whole fucking Castle mess." He was dead serious. "Promise me."

"What?" she asked.

"You want a future? Start putting us first."

—

Raf's backpack was in the lab, but he wasn't.

Lily pulled out her cell phone.

"Angela?" she began. "We need to talk."

"We're doing that," Angela said testily.

"Face to face."

"How fortunate. I'm right outside."

Lily peered through the blind, then went out to join her.

"You lied to me," Angela said. "And clumsily."

"I'm sorry. And I'll pay for the dress." Behind Angela, Raf was sauntering down the block. He had on a new T-shirt and was carrying a paper bag. When he saw Lily, he broke into a jig. Shifting to block Angela's view, she motioned him to stay back. "How'd you know about Raf?"

"You think Sasha and I don't talk?" Angela said. Raf was standing stock still, and pedestrians detoured around him. "Why do you think I brought you on?"

"My eye?" Lily asked.

"Fuck your eye! It's to keep me honest, and you're doing a piss poor job of that."

"That's why I need Raf." As Lily spoke, he took another giant step forward. His T-shirt read *Curbside Pickup*, and he stood teetering on one foot. Busking was in his blood.

"And?" Angela said.

"*Schuylerhaugh* can't travel," Lily replied.

"Tell me something new."

"It isn't a real Cole."

Angela belted out a laugh. "Welcome back!" Paul had been wrong: she truly was a buccaneer's daughter. "Benjy's ancestor was a lesser Schuyler. Even at $25 a pop, I doubt he could attract Thomas Cole. What do you want to do, Lily?"

"Tell the Rensselaer to cancel the insurance." Behind Angela's back, Raf flashed a thumb's-up. "Benjy can deliver the keynote with slides. If they ask, we'll say it's attributed to Cole."

Raf opened his bag, and a yeasty aroma floated out. Angela spun around. He held out a pretzel studded with enough rock salt to melt a New York sidewalk. "Beer—or schnapps?" he asked.

Angela's eyes narrowed, then she guffawed. "You're on the payroll!"

Two of a kind.

"He needs a place to stay," Lily said. "I'd offer my couch—"

"Nonsense." Angela tore into the pretzel. "I can use a man around the house."

Chapter Thirty-Nine

"Slick move back there," Lily said after Angela had left.

"The pretzels?" Raf shrugged. "Luck."

"Bullshit!" His bag had held three. "How did you know she'd come?"

He winked. "You think Sasha and I don't talk?"

Lily sank into her chair.

"No need for a condition report now." Raf gazed at *Schuylerhaugh* with a cockeyed fondness. "Even a bad artist cared."

"Yeah."

Now they could start tackling the Foundation's off-site storage facility. It was crammed with enough hits and near-misses to keep them busy—and Gina and Michel sniffing around—forever. Maybe she could lure Matt over from her old lab.

"Forgetting something?" Raf asked.

I promised him a murder. "They're handling it."

"Your FBI guy and Johnson?" he scoffed.

"I've come within a hair of losing Paul and my career, Raf. If the killer's at CT—"

"*If?*"

"Johnson's smart." Bowles liked the old detective, and she'd promised Paul.

"So much for three dead people." Raf banged around the lab, looking for materials to ship the painting back to Benjy. "But what about that poor schmuck in Phoenix?"

"Forget the dioramas, Raf."

Lily unlocked the back room. Like the Foundation's off-site facility, it was stocked with enough materials to create and restore a thousand fantasies, when all *Schuylerhaugh* needed now was foamcore, acid-free paper and a sturdy crate. But the room's compact efficiency was formidable in its own right; it would have impressed a decluttering coach like Bliss Byrd, a girl trying to fit her life into a micro-mini studio like Demi, or a master architect-turned-toymaker like Adam Castle. But an architect needed a drafting table and tools. "Where does he really work?" she mused.

"Adam?" Raf rooted around a shelf. "You said his studio was in his garage."

The Castles' garage abutted their house, but when Adam led them on his grand tour, they'd entered it from the outside. He'd bombarded Trudi with a punch list; why didn't he add an access door? And she didn't remember seeing a security keypad or motion-activated floodlight. Sloppy of him—or arrogant?

"Let's take a ride," Lily said.

—

Castle Keep backed onto an alley and its backyard was fenced. There was no sign of Eve's Mercedes or Adam's pickup. "The garage has a back window," she told Raf.

"Jeez, Lily! What if there's a camera?"

"Pretend you're looking for a dog," she replied.

"Inside the frigging garage?"

"I'm not asking you to break in." For now. "Just look."

"And if I'm busted?"

"Bowles will bail us out." But she could tell Raf was warming to the plan. Sasha was right: crime must be in his blood.

"I'm starting to see a big simple—"

"Pretend you're rotating a cube or sphere," she coaxed. "We just need to know if the worktable and shelves take up the entire space."

Raf opened the car door and gracefully hopped the fence. He hoisted himself onto the window ledge and peered in. For what felt like an eon, his wiry frame clung there. Then he jumped down and crept along the back of the house. Three minutes later he dusted off his hands and leapt into the Prius.

"The wall behind the shelves looks like plaster." He was breathing heavily, more from excitement than exertion. "There's six dead feet between it and the den. Now let's get the fuck out of here!"

———

Back at the lab, they made short work of the cold cuts. Lily let Raf finish his sandwich before broaching her plan.

"No," he said.

"I'll go in with you," she promised.

"This is insane, Lily."

"We have to see what's in that room."

"And if it's nothing," he argued, "a structural anomaly?"

"Then we'll know we've done what we can."

Raf peered across the desk. "Where's your FBI guy?"

"Out of town," Lily said.

"You could wait till he gets back," he suggested slyly. "He ain't Spiderman, but I bet he's used a crowbar. Or is he too straight to break the law?"

"Paul's no longer with the FBI."

"But an art historian can risk his neck!" He was loving this. "What's wrong with this picture?"

"I promised him I'd stay out of it," she said meekly.

"That's not all, is it?" Raf demanded.

"Paul's fixated on Frank." Lily set down her sandwich and explained why.

"DARPA, huh?" Raf said when she was done. "Maybe he's right. But peeking in a garage is one thing; breaking into an occupied house is out."

"Agreed."

Lily phoned Angela.

"What now?" Angela groaned.

"I have a favor to ask."

"Don't press your luck." But she sounded intrigued.

"Throw a dinner," Lily asked.

"For the new boy wonder?"

"The Castles."

"I already did," Angela said. "You were there, remember?"

How stylish and charming they'd seemed that night! Eve with that frightful baby doll, Adam with the secret room in Angela's library. "But he didn't get a chance to pitch remodeling your place."

"How thoughtful of you," Angela said drily. "When?"

"Tomorrow evening, early." While it was still light outside.

"Is Paul—"

"We're not coming," Lily said. "It's for your friend Bliss Byrd."

"Not another word." Angela's were clipped. "When do you want them here?"

Chapter Forty

The Castles drove off in Eve's Mercedes.

"Damn!" Lily had been hoping they'd walk. A breeze was picking up; if Eve wanted a scarf, she might send Adam home for one. "Fifteen minutes max," she warned Raf as she dropped him off in the alley.

By Lily's second time around the block, he'd climbed through the garage window and cracked the door open from the inside. She parked three houses away and waited for a man and dog to round the corner. Then she slipped into the garage.

"What're we looking for?" Raf whispered.

"A door." Metal shelves were bolted to the wall abutting the Castles' den at two-foot intervals. Studs. She turned on her phone's flashlight and played it at eye level. The shelves were two feet deep and stacked with plastic bins. "We have to take everything down."

"In eight minutes?"

Lily ran the flash across the cement floor. Halfway down the length of the wall was a small stain—oil, or paint. Directly above, one section of shelving ended and another began. Between the sections was a small gap. Wedging her fingers into the gap, she gently pried the shelves apart and pulled outward. They started to swing open like the façade on Angela's baby dollhouse.

"Grab that bin!" she shouted.

Raf caught it before it fell. "Tiny trees!"

"No time."

They cleared the shelves and swung the frame the rest of the way open, exposing the bare wall behind it. Lily gave Raf the light and ran her fingers along the plaster. At hip height she felt a panel with a latch like an airplane lavatory's. She raised it and slid the bolt. Blackness gaped.

"Have you read Poe?" Raf asked.

"Give me that light." It sounded braver than she felt. The space was six feet deep and ten long. A cord dangled from the ceiling.

"I'll wait in the car," Raf said.

"After coming this far?" she cajoled. "Some historian you are!"

"Do I get hazard pay?" he whined.

"Awfully pushy for a new hire."

Raf squeezed in after her. Lily pulled the cord and a high-intensity ceiling light flared to reveal a worktable and a chair. She switched off her flash and blinked rapidly to let her eyes adjust. Outside a dog barked.

"No blueprints," Raf said. "Can we go?"

Slowly her eyes focused "Raf, look…"

Cautiously he turned back to the table. "Dolls?"

They were a six-inch man and a five-inch woman. The man had dark hair and an action figure's physique. Instead of tights and a cape, he wore a well-cut suit whose lapels were a touch wide. The woman was blonde, in a clingy black dress with an off-the-shoulder neckline and ballerina sleeves. Her eyes were inquiring and her expression determined. Lily's blood ran cold. Adam's next victims didn't have to be in Phoenix.

"You," Raf said softly, "but the wrong dress. And your FBI guy would never wear that suit. It's from the Seventies."

Lily pointed to a metal tray. Nail scissors, dental pick, mascara wand. The wand was loaded with grey pigment. "He's working on the hair," she said calmly. "He hasn't decided how old to make them."

The dog barked again, sounding closer.

"Better go," Raf said.

"Yeah." She reached for the dolls.

"Lily, don't…"

The dog growled.

She thrust the dolls in her bag, extinguished the light and closed the door. With Raf holding her phone in his teeth, they quickly put the bins back and swung the shelves into place. The flashlight glanced off the large table, where the Tudor was now center stage. Adam had furnished the living room with a miniature wingchair and ottoman. A side table held a folded paper and spectacles, as if the man of the house had just stepped out. To warm his feet, Adam had added the fireplace.

Raf let out a low whistle. "Phoenix."

Not Phoenix, Denver. "We've got to go."

He shook his head in wonder. "But it's so real."

"Raf—"

"Lily, look." He peered at the hearth with the tiny logs. "There's even a key to ignite the gas!"

In his excitement, he tilted the flash and lit the diorama's floor. Yellow chalk silhouetted two figures: a six-inch man with broad shoulders and hand outstretched, with a puddle around his head; and a five-inch woman with a dark pool spreading from her chest. Raf backed away. "Let's get out of here."

Lily looked at the foliage surrounding the Tudor. True to his promise, Adam had torn out the pfitzers and planted hydrangeas. She wiggled a bush. It wasn't glued. Was the path attached, or just laid out? She slung her bag over her shoulder. "We're relocating this."

"To Phoenix?" Raf asked.

"Not that far. Now give me a hand."

Reluctantly he stepped back. They each took an end. At the count of three, they lifted the diorama. The furniture was glued and the structure surprisingly light. With the back seat of the Prius folded down, there'd be room for it in the cargo hold.

"What about the hydrangeas?" Raf asked.

"Leave them. Is the coast clear?"

He peeked outside and nodded. No dog.

"Just a sec." Lily fished in her bag for paper and pen.

Come get me, she scribbled. *You know where!* She propped the note between two hydrangeas.

Raf raised his end of the diorama again. "How do you know Adam will come?"

"It's his totem."

Chapter Forty-One

Paul sat across from Frank Gould in his blindingly bright office in downtown Phoenix. "Thanks for seeing us, professor."

Frank leaned back in his leather swivel chair and grinned. His white polo showed off toned biceps and a buff torso. *Must have a helluva golf swing*, Paul thought. The window behind Frank framed a set from a Hollywood Western: too-blue sky, scrubby valley, half-assed mountains encircling the city. "I'd hoped to continue our dialogue, Paul," he said, "but I'm guessing you're not here to discuss the psychic blows dwellings inflict."

Next to Paul, Johnson fidgeted. They'd flown in last night, and he'd taken one breath and groused about his asthma. This morning he overslept and missed breakfast. Now he eyed the little bowl on Frank's desk. "Candy?" Frank jiggled the bowl at him. "Gum?"

"I'm good," Johnson said.

"We're here about CT," Paul said.

"Marvelous program!" Frank's eyes twinkled. "Cleared any old cases lately?"

"We're hoping you'll help," Paul replied.

"I'll put on my forensic shrink hat."

Johnson smiled sourly. "Decluttering coach blown to shit in a sardine can. Art collector's brains splattered over gallery-type walls. Hotshot lawyer clubbed in a hot tub. Ring a bell, prof?"

Frank laughed. "Like a cell phone about to go dead. You have a poet's ear, detective, but what's unique about those sites?"

"Geez, I dunno… They're dead ringers for CT dioramas?"

Frank genially waved off a couple of students hovering outside. Glass doors and a pristine desktop made him appear to have nothing to hide. Instead of commendations, combat photos or DOD memorabilia, over his credenza a pair of small abstracts hung. Expensively mounted, they were positioned directly above two framed photographs.

Paul kept it light. "CT's your brainchild."

"I don't consult with Eve on scripts," Frank replied.

Bingo. Paul leaned forward. "But you saw the dioramas in Denver."

"Cook's tour." Frank winked at Johnson. "Desk sarge let me in. But I can't talk about the Castles. I counseled them."

"In Eugene?" Paul asked.

Frank held his gaze. "Carl Peters is a good friend."

"He thinks you were set up. By whom?"

"Who cares?"

Paul resisted the bait. "You move around a lot, don't you, Frank? UCLA, Carnegie Mellon, Tulane, Eugene…"

Frank shrugged. "The life of an academic."

"Still, it must be hard to set down roots."

"Gee, I never thought of it that way. But maybe that's why my investments are portable." Frank chuckled, and his eyes flitted to the wall above the credenza. "When's your flight?"

Johnson snorted. "Adam Castle rat you out?"

In the window behind Frank, clouds were building.

"What do you think of Adam?" Paul pressed.

"Damn fine architect." Frank couldn't resist. "Eve upped his game."

Smug prick. If Frank was using CT for research, or he and Eve wanted Adam out of the picture, they'd never admit it. As Frank turned back to the window, Paul glanced at the credenza. One photo was Frank in combat fatigues and Black Ops shades, kneeling beside a short-haired black dog on a leash. German Shepherd but smaller, with pointy ears and eyes just this side of crazy. Bin Laden and SEAL Team Six.

"Belgian Malinois?" Paul asked.

"Buddy," Frank said without looking. "They let me bring him home."

"Smart dog." *Like the house in Portland?*

Frank turned and smirked. "Dogs are smart. Houses aren't." He stood. "Not to be inhospitable—"

Paul rose and went to the credenza. The other photo was of a younger Frank in a tux, with his arm around a pretty girl with flowing red hair and a sexy gap in her teeth. She posed with him under a canopy of roses, in a lacy white dress.

"The ex that got away," Frank said sardonically. "Seen enough, Paul?"

Fuck.

Lily was right. If the killer was at CT, it had to be Adam. The airport was ten minutes away. But there was something strange about the credenza: the juxtaposition of the photos on the otherwise empty surface, the careful placement of the abstracts above them. Almost like an altar—or a trophy wall. Frank turned back to the window, and Paul whipped out his cell and took a quick shot.

Frank gestured at the clouds. "Better hightail it to Kansas before the black blizzard hits."

"Blizzard?" Johnson asked.

Paul hit *send*. Frank turned sharply.

"Just calling an Uber," Paul explained.

Frank laughed. "Assuming your flight isn't cancelled."

Paul looked out the window. Over the mountains an immense vertical wall had risen. The mile-high mass roiled and seethed like a tsunami, then slowly began moving towards them.

"Tornado?" Paul asked.

"Haboob," Frank said.

"Beg pardon?" Johnson said.

Frank rolled his eyes. "Windstorm."

"How long does it last?" Johnson asked.

"Five minutes or a lifetime."

Johnson blanched. "I ain't afraid—"

Frank shrugged. "You should be, but I'm a pessimist."

The Western morphed into a sci-fi flick. The wall of debris swallowed the mountains and rolled downslope, obliterating everything in its path. Blackness erased scrub and seemed to reduce buildings to toys. Cars sped away.

"The dust carries heavy metals and pesticides," Frank said. "Not to mention Valley Fever."

"Valley—?" Johnson asked.

"Fungal infection from spores." Frank smiled drily. "Try not to breathe."

—

"Where's that Uber!" Johnson shouted.

"What?" The wind howled like a train.

"Car!"

A bucket of sand hit Paul in the face. His eyes and nose and mouth filled with grit. He couldn't see. His arm tightened around Johnson.

Fucking stupid way to die.

He gripped his phone.

Blindly he tapped keys.

i luv

It was over.

Chapter Forty-Two

On the parkway outside the Tudor, traffic ebbed.

"This is a really bad idea," Raf muttered.

"So you've said." Lily turned from the window. "Relax."

"A thousand ways this could end, and not a damn one of them's good." Raf momentarily brightened. "Maybe Adam won't come."

"I told you, this diorama's sacred." They'd set it in front of the hearth.

"But they auctioned off the others."

Lily shook her head. "The Tudor is the mother ship."

Headlights from the parkway flickered, briefly bringing the chandelier's antlers alive. This better be over fast.

"What if Eve comes too?" Raf fretted.

"She won't." Lily tried to sound confident. "Adam can't let her see a dead doll wearing her dress."

Raf gazed at the hearth. "That's some big-ass fireplace," he said queasily. "Big enough to stew a goat."

"Medieval chic." But it creeped her out, too. Who needed a walk-in fireplace these days? "Your turn."

Raf took her place at the window. For a moment Lily wondered if it had been fair to drag him into this. She glanced at the text Angela had sent five minutes ago. *Lift off!* Adam had left Angela's. When he got home, he might not kiss his dolls goodnight, but he'd check on the diorama. This would all be over soon.

She texted Paul again. *Where R U?*

Still no answer. Her last calls had gone to voicemail that disconnected. She pictured him in a D.C. bar, schmoozing with clients and smoothing over awkward questions about taking over for Hunter. But time had run out for them all. After Adam's outburst in this very house two nights ago, Eve must know her husband was losing it; and if the Castles were keeping score, this was Adam's last chance to beat her at the game meant to keep their marriage alive. His last shot at proving he was a better man than Frank.

Lily settled into the wingchair. The streetlight shone through the leaded glass window onto the diorama. When she and Raf absconded with it, the plan had sounded good. Was it too late to load it back in the Prius and call it a night? If she did, Johnson would be the only hope that Phoenix couple—whoever they were—would have to avoid becoming victims of a murder-suicide staged in their own life-sized Tudor. Or had she and Paul been too good an opportunity for Adam to pass up? His dolls were almost perfect; except for the man's wide lapels, and with a few more grey hairs, he was a dead ringer for Paul. Dressing the female doll like Eve but giving her Lily's expression was a message and a taunt. She had to bring it to a head.

Ping! Paul?

She grabbed her phone.

From Angela. *A back E 4got bag*

Lily looked at Raf. At the sight of his rooster hair and guileless face, her affection for him surged. But with it came a shiv of remorse. Breaking in was impulsive, taking the dolls worse. Stealing the diorama was the point of no return. Suddenly she knew Sasha was wrong. Raf wasn't cut out for this at all.

Ping. Angela again. *Nroute.*

This was for real.

"Go," she said.

"What?" Raf said.

"Take the Prius." It was parked behind the house.

He ignored the outstretched key.

Lily smiled reassuringly. "I'm just getting Adam to confess. He wants to be caught, but he won't do it if you're here."

Raf shook his head stubbornly. "What if he brings a weapon?"

"He won't use it." They'd been through this. "And it's safer if you're not here, Raf."

"Safer?"

She thought fast. "Murder-suicide requires two people. There's no point killing just me."

Raf frowned. "What am I—*nobody*? I'm not leaving without you, Lily."

Piss him off. "Your work's done, Raf."

He sighed with relief. "I'm glad you agree. I've been saying all night this plan's insane."

Double or nothing.

"You don't get it, Raf. I don't need you anymore." Lily pretended to scroll through her phone. Obligingly it pinged. She looked at the screen sightlessly to avoid the pain in his eyes. "See? Paul's on his way."

"Yeah?" Raf shouted. "Where the fuck was he when you needed someone to jump a fence and break into a garage?"

Lily stared back at him, willing her gaze not to falter. Paul had almost died saving her back in that killer's filthy shed. She wasn't about to let that happen to Raf now. *Make it really hurt.* "Go back to whoever she was," she said scornfully. "If you're not too much of an asshole, maybe she'll take you back."

Raf stared at her incredulously.

"I mean it, Raf. Take the fucking car and go!" Lily flung the keys at him.

Catching them with one hand, he gazed at her with contempt. "I never figured you for a bitch, Lily. But if you want to get yourself killed, I'm not going to stay and watch."

He took the back door. A moment later, Lily heard the crunch of the Prius' tires on gravel.

Hands trembling, she took the dolls from her bag. She turned on her flash and examined them more closely. They were posable, made from a flexible polymer—iconic but all too human. The woman had big breasts. Lily twisted her at the waist. Her bodice gaped and the skirt was too full. The man was ripped like Super Man. She unbent his arm and the suit fit better. But Raf was right; even if Paul were Clark Kent, he'd never wear such wide lapels. Why were they dressed this way? She looked at the woman again. Her temples had strands of grey.

Lily put away the dolls and looked past the diorama to the hearth. In the scripting, which had come first—this Tudor or the diorama? The wingchair she sat in wasn't here two nights ago, or the ottoman. Maybe Adam kept a tiny set in stock and expedited Wayfair for life-sized ones. The side table also seemed new, but the reading glasses and folded paper were as dated as the dolls' attire. The paper was turned to classifieds, or—

Why a Tudor? *Anglo aristocracy for the middle class.* Maybe this wasn't about Paul and her—or some unlucky couple in Phoenix—at all. Suddenly she yearned for Paul. Why didn't he answer his phone? The text she'd bullshitted Raf about was *Game on!* from Angela.

She scrolled her e-mails. One had come in from Paul. No subject or words, just a photo of a couple of small paintings over a credenza in an office. She enlarged the shot and focused on the painting to the left. An indigo starburst exploded in its upper corner. The companion piece had a smaller burst and a longer tail. Earlier, less assured versions of Hunter's abstracts, the ones Bruce Kemp made worthless by flooding the market. Scrolling down to the credenza, she saw a photo of Frank Gould in combat fatigues with a black dog, and another of him with a girl in a wedding dress. Flowing red hair, gap in her teeth—was that Bliss Byrd?

She fled an earlier control-freak husband, Angela had told her.

Lily had been going after the marionette instead of the one pulling the strings.

A flicker on the wall—a car was pulling up front. The headlights were higher than the ones on a Mercedes. Adam's pickup.

He was alone.

Chapter Forty-Three

The streetlight made Adam's shadow larger than life.

"I knew you'd come around, Lily." He leaned over the back of the wingchair, his breath on her hair. "If nothing else, this place is a fabulous teardown. Where's Paul?"

"On his way."

"Really? Angela said he was out of town." He laughed nastily. "Is he with Hunter's clients? The firm tried to foist me off on an associate, but my Cherry Creek commission's dead." Empty-handed, he rounded the chair and gestured at the diorama. "Couldn't resist, eh? You jumped the gun on my housewarming gift." He stooped to inspect it. There was nothing in his back pockets.

"What about Phoenix?" she asked.

"Don't need it now." Adam turned, and in the streetlight's glare his gaze was black and flat. Was that the last thing Hunter and Bruce saw? Thank God Raf was gone. This was her mess—not his. Or Paul's.

"I'll see if Paul's landed," Lily said. But if that photo was from Frank's office, he must be in Phoenix. Calmly reaching for her phone, she pretended to scroll for messages and hit *video*. Adam grabbed the phone and threw it in the hearth.

His voice was low and coarse. "Give me those dolls."

Stooping for her bag, Lily scanned for a weapon to use. The fireplace logs were scaly and grey, too dense to burn. If she could distract Adam, could she grab one and stun him? She pulled out the female doll. *Get him talking.*

"I thought you were a perfectionist," she said.

"I am."

"Her skirt's too wide," she said scornfully.

"Not for dancing."

She shook her head with pity. "Forty years ago, maybe. Now, Demi—"

Adam snorted. "She just needed a robe."

"Like Bliss Byrd?"

He chuckled. "Your scripts are way more fun than Eve's."

Lily bent the doll at the waist. The curtsy exposed her tits.

"Leave her alone!" he cried.

"Demi and Bliss, Adam. What'd Eve tell you—no room for a man?"

He stepped back. "Demi suffocated, remember? And Bliss' house blew up." He giggled. "Talk about decluttering—"

Tires crunched on gravel. Lily's heart leapt. Paul? She pulled the man doll from her bag. "And Bruce Kemp. You and Eve were at his soirée, right?"

"So?" Adam stared at the doll. In the shadows behind him, Lily thought she saw something move.

She kept talking. "You're an artist." Nodding in the direction of the doorway, she made the man doll nod too. "I bet you felt for that young artist whose career Bruce destroyed." She stroked the doll's lapels. "Now, Hunter—"—*Paul*—"wouldn't be caught dead in this suit."

Adam lunged. "Give him to me!"

Lily held the doll tight.

Adam went to the grate. When he turned, he was holding a box cutter. Industrial size, heavy plastic handle and grips. He waved it at her. She scrabbled for the newspaper to deflect the blade. Time it right and maybe—Adam advanced with the box cutter.

From the shadows behind him, she saw someone nod. Paul?

Go for it.

"Did you catch Eve with Hunter?" she taunted. Adam stopped short. "Or was that what she made you think? Must've been something big to get you to kill the guy who held your future in his hands."

Adam squinted, then a look of amusement crossed his face. "She was right, you really don't have a clue."

Lily looked down at the doll's bulging torso. Not Hunter—or even Paul. The folded newspaper in her hand was the *The Pittsburgh Gazette.* Obits. No need to check the date. Were Ed and Mary Castle the man with the wide lapels, the woman in the too-full dress? Their Tudor must have been a death trap, but damned if this would be!

Make him turn on Eve.

Lily rose. "What happened to your parents, Adam?"

"None of—"

The shadow moved again. "Was it gas, like Bliss? I bet that was Eve's idea, too."

"You fucking—"

"Were your parents the first?"

"Don't answer, Adam." Eve stepped from the doorway and gently took his box cutter away. "Shush…" she soothed. With her free hand, she caressed his cheek.

Smiling, she raised a gun at Lily.

"Congratulations. You're CT's first suicide."

Chapter Forty-Four

No headlights on the parkway, no sporty Prius crunching on gravel. Raf wasn't coming. Or Paul. Or Bowles. It was just her and the Castles. Lily looked at Eve. She'd said it after Demi's diorama, that very first night.

He commits the crimes. I write the scripts.

Her and Frank.

"New script?" Lily asked.

Eve smiled enigmatically. Like a designer unveiling a Christmas window, she threw the wall switch. The antlered chandelier lit and the diorama sprang to life. With three walls and the ceiling open, and the immense hearth as a backdrop, it was a miniature theater. Any moment tiny actors would take the stage to enact the Tudor script. But now Lily knew she herself was just a bit actor, because this wasn't about her and Paul. It wasn't even about Ed or Mary Castle. It was about modeling an obedient universe.

Adam had retrieved the box cutter. From the wings, he held it loosely against his leg. Anticipation lit his face. *Domestic scenes are deadly terrain*, Eve had said. *Enacting them on a tiny stage lets kids conquer the universe. The wonder is more adults don't....* Did Frank have Eve play out her childhood dramas?

"Adam wants to kill a man," Lily said.

"He'll do what he's told."

Anything for Eve. Not just the screenwriter—the director. She had to break Frank's hold over them both. *Flip the script.*

Lily handed Eve the woman doll.

Eve gently straightened her out. "Oh, Adam, you remembered Mary's dress." The box cutter beat a tattoo against his leg. The second he loosened his grip—Eve gave him the doll. "You know where to start."

Adam obediently went to the diorama. Stooping, he peered into the kitchen. For the first time, Lily noticed the old-fashioned porcelain sink and cupboard with tiny ceramic dishes. Adam posed Mary at the sink.

"Hovering," Eve murmured, "always taking his side. While you lie in bed trembling, seeing and hearing more than you should. And waiting..."

Adam tore the cupboard from the wall and smashed the dishes in the sink. But the gesture was robotic. This really wasn't about him either.

"Don't listen to her," Lily said. "It's not Mary—"

"Shut up!" Eve pointed the gun at her. "Give me Ed."

Lily gave her the male doll. How could she have thought it was Paul?

Bending Ed at waist and knees, Eve sat him in the diorama's wingchair and placed the newspaper in his hands. "Obsessed with each other, no room for a brilliant, sensitive little child." The script Frank must've used on her. "Do it, Adam."

Adam cocked Ed's head. Was he making him listen to Eve, or to Mary in the kitchen? He slowly unbent Ed from the chair, raised the doll's hands to its elbows and balled its fingers into tiny fists.

"Do it," Eve ordered. Her murders—or Frank's?

"Stop!" Lily cried.

Adam looked up.

"They're not your parents," Lily said.

Eve shook her head scornfully and gave him the gun. "You missed your chance with Ed and Mary, but you can still make it come out right."

Commit Frank's murders so I don't have to.

"Don't—" Lily begged.

"Prove yourself to me," Eve wheedled Adam. "One last time and you win. Be a bigger man than Frank." *Win me back by killing the people he hates.*

Adam squeezed his eyes shut. "Did you ever love me?" he whispered.

"Remember Hunter?" Eve scowled. "He dissed you by palming you off on an associate. I got him in the tub, and you did the rest. Now kill her!"

Did Adam realize he himself could be joining Lily on the floor?

"Do it!" Eve cried.

Adam reluctantly motioned Lily to the fireplace. "I can't—"

Eve's face hardened with contempt. Two quick strides brought her to Adam's side. She slapped him in the face. "Bliss was easy. Luring her with the cat, standing by while she screamed and banged her fists bloody on that door. Stupid obsession, that tiny house." Her voice dripped with scorn. "Nobody's ever taken you seriously, Adam. Even with a gun to his head, Bruce tried to buy you off. Frank would never let him get away with that." Another slap rang out. "Now be a man!"

The big simple value pattern was Eve and Frank.

Eve's first victims must have been her parents. She'd been raised by that hated granny with the dollhouse and the demeaning mantra, *Girl's play prepares you for women's work.* After killing her parents, how that message must have stung! But Eve had met her match with Frank. Her lover, CT's godfather, Adam's rival—the eternal elephant on the Castles' rug. By getting them to do his dirty work, Frank wasn't just master of their tiny universe. He was God.

Adam finally remembered his lines. "On the floor!" he ordered.

Lily got to her knees.

He cocked the gun at her head.

"Hey!" a familiar voice called.

They turned to the doorway.

Raf stood there with the Prius' keys in his hand.

"Well, well," Eve said. "A murder-suicide after all." Was she disappointed? Her last step would be killing Adam, but now that final piece of Frank's plan had to wait. "Drop the keys!"

Raf set the keys down and scooted over to the hearth.

"On the floor!" Adam ordered.

Raf dropped to his knees and crawled to Lily. He looked at her urgently. She tried to read the message in his eyes. Not regret, but—

Raf opened his hand. The gas valve key and a box of matches. He slipped the matches to her. "One," he whispered.

She sprang to her feet.

"Two!" he cried.

She struck a match and flipped it in the hearth. The log didn't light.

Eve grabbed at the gun.

Lily struck another match and aimed for the grate.

Another.

Then another.

Whoosh! Flames shot from the dense logs.

"Three!" Lily and Raf picked up the diorama and heaved it in.

Adam reared back in horror.

Fire tickled the Tudor. It flared and burst into flames.

With a cry of rage, Adam leapt in after it. Flames licked his legs and darted to his hair. He grabbed the Tudor and hugged it. He turned to them with a grotesque smile.

His mouth froze in a hideous scream.

Then came an enormous roar.

Chapter Forty-Five

"I'm never taking you to a DPD event again," Paul said.

"But Johnson and I are such friends! Maybe if I bring chocolates…" On cue, the chocolatier emerged from Stargazer's backroom with a tray of truffles. At the counter, the barista was steaming milk, and the air swirled with the whir and scent of coffee grinding. Outside, golden leaves were falling and the sky was a hard bright blue. "I like this place."

"You'd better. We're becoming regulars."

"I mean the neighborhood," Lily said.

"That too."

The barista waved to Paul. He brought their lattes to the table and unfurled the floorplan. "I still want a den."

"And a sunroom." Lily took the truffle Paul gave her and bit into it. It was dusted with cocoa and had a ganache center. "Can you believe the Castles' house hasn't sold?" They'd passed the Tiffany blue *TR For Sale* sign on the way over. "I hope Trudi isn't losing her touch."

Paul laughed. "Don't worry. Unlike our new scrape, your condo isn't a crime scene." She'd listed it with Trudi, who'd gotten them a steal on the parkway Tudor because the chimney was the only thing left. Elena didn't even need to wave a smudge stick; they were rebuilding from the ground up. "Thank God the doors blew out," he said. "I still can't believe you and Raf walked away."

They weren't the only ones who'd walked.

Lily was still furious about the meeting with Johnson four months earlier when Bliss Byrd's case had been closed. "Misadventure," he'd said, "like your own little brush with death. What were you and Feldman really doing in that vacant house?"

"I told you," she'd replied. "The Castles lured us there."

"Give me more than some half-baked—"

"But Eve confessed!"

"Confessed?" he wheezed. "All you got is her accusing her husband of crimes."

"What about the gun?" Lily demanded.

Johnson pulled out an inhaler. "Registered to Adam, not her."

"But Raf—"

"—saw it in his hand, not hers." He puffed on his inhaler. "Ballistics matched it to Kemp and Merritt. We're closing them, too."

"How convenient," she'd said. "What about their parents?"

"Adam's?" Johnson had sucked harder on his inhaler. "Ed and Mary Castle died in a highway crash in 1986."

"And Eve's parents?"

"Kitchen fire when she was eight," he'd muttered.

"What a surprise!" Lily had almost pitied Frank.

Now the chocolatier swung by with a fresh tray of samples. Lily chose one and gave it to Paul. He looked up hopefully from the floorplan. "Workshop in the garage?"

"A detail." Not their big simple value pattern.

"Hmmn?" he said.

Her phone pinged. Another Instagram from Eve. *CT's gone international!* read the caption with the photo of her and Frank in front of a grand hacienda with that strange-looking black dog straining on a leash. *Come visit our castle in Spain.* Eve had got one thing right: houses were just objects. But hadn't Adam said something about her hating dogs?

Maybe even God needed to hedge his bets.

Lily deleted the Instagram and reached for her bag. "I won't be long," she promised.

"On Saturday?" Paul groaned.

"Raf's knee-deep in inventory."

"I'll try not to be jealous," he said.

She bent and kissed him.

"See you at home."

Acknowledgments

A heartfelt thanks to my editor, Mark Chimsky, and partners in crime Victoria Becker, Jan Prince and Janette MacDonald. And to my husband, John, whose enduring love and support are my greatest object lessons.

The godmother of crime scene dioramas was Frances Glessner Lee. To learn more about her fascinating life and work, read *The Nutshell Studies of Unexplained Death*, by Corinne May Botz.

The image on the cover of *Object Lessons* is adapted from a 1903 photo taken by renowned French criminalist and crime scene photographer Alphonse Bertillon. The woman in the photo was Madame Berthe de Brienne, a wealthy Parisienne who was strangled during a burglary in her flat on Rue Chalgrin. Her killer was sentenced to penal servitude for life.

About the Author

Stephanie Kane is a lawyer and award-winning crime writer. She has lectured on money laundering and white-collar crime in Eastern Europe and given workshops on writing technique throughout the U.S. She lives in Denver with her husband and two black cats.

For more information, please visit *www.writerkane.com.*

If you enjoyed *Object Lessons,* please post a review. Reviews help books reach new readers!